# The Wings of Ecstasy

# THE WINGS OF ECSTASY

## Barbara Cartland

G.K. Hall & Co. • Chivers Press
Thorndike, Maine USA   Bath, England

This Large Print edition is published by G.K. Hall & Co., USA
and by Chivers Press, England.

Published in 1999 in the U.S. by arrangement with
International Book Marketing, Ltd.

Published in 1999 in the U.K. by arrangement with
Cartland Promotions.

U.S.  Softcover     0-7838-8609-8   (Paperback Series Edition)
U.K.  Hardcover     0-7540-3799-1   (Chivers Large Print)
U.K.  Softcover     0-7540-3800-9   (Camden Large Print)

The text of this Large Print edition is unabridged.
Other aspects of the book may vary from the original edition.

Set in 16 pt. Plantin by Rick Gundberg.

Printed in the United States on permanent paper.

**British Library Cataloguing in Publication Data available**

**Library of Congress Cataloging in Publication Data**

Cartland, Barbara, 1902–
    The wings of ecstasy / Barbara Cartland.
        p.    cm.
    ISBN 0-7838-8609-8 (lg. print : sc : alk. paper)
    1. Large type books.  I. Title.
    [PR6005.A765W56 1999]
    823′.912—dc21                                                99-20125

# Author's Note

Although Wiedenstein is a fictitious country the details about Paris during the Second Empire are correct.

The word *demi-mondaine* was coined by Dumas *fils* to describe the world of the *déclassés* — a world which began where the legal wife ends and finishes where the mistress begins.

In a play by Barrière one of the characters says: "it is neither the aristocracy nor the bourgeoisie, but it floats on the ocean of Paris".

There were a dozen courtesans, the Queens of their profession who were known as *le garde*. Each woman considered her beauty her capital and made it pay fantastic dividends. La Païva, born in a Moscow ghetto, wore two million francs worth of diamonds, pearls and precious stones and was called the "great debauchée of the century".

In March 1871, one year later than this novel, when the Prussians entered Paris, La Païva's lover Prince Henchel von Donnersmarch in full uniform watched his compatriots march past.

# Chapter One
# 1869

The Arch-Duke of Wiedenstein was engrossed in the newspaper and the rest of his family who were breakfasting with him were silent.

It was always a somewhat uncomfortable meal as they were never certain in what sort of mood their father would be.

Prince Kendric took the last piece of toast and having piled it with butter and marmalade, English fashion, ate it quickly and pushed back his chair.

As he did so his mother, the Arch-Duchess, looked up from the letter she had been reading, and gave a significant cough.

She also looked fixedly at the newspaper which concealed her husband, but there was no response.

"Leopold," she said in a voice that was bound to attract his attention.

The Arch-Duke looked over his newspaper in a manner which showed he was irritated at being interrupted, caught his wife's eye and said:

"Yes, yes, of course!"

Prince Kendric and his twin sister Princess Marie-Thérèse, who in the family circle was always called "Zena", stared at their father apprehensively.

They had the feeling that they were about to be given a lecture, which was nothing unusual.

The Arch-Duke put the newspaper down slowly on the table and took off his spectacles.

He never wore them in public if he could help it because he thought they spoilt his image.

He had been, and still was, a very handsome man. In fact, the coins of Wiedenstein hardly did him justice.

All his life there had been women to tell him that his looks were irresistible, which was something he had attempted unsuccessfully to keep secret from his wife.

"Your father wishes to speak to you," the Arch-Duchess said unnecessarily in a low tone.

Prince Kendric wished he had left the room earlier, but even if he had tried he was certain his mother would have prevented him from escaping.

The Arch-Duke cleared his throat.

"I have received," he said slowly and ponderously, "a report from your Tutors on your educational progress over these last three months."

He paused because he was looking at his daughter and thinking that she was looking particularly attractive this morning, and it diverted his mind from what he was about to say.

Then his eyes crossed the table to look at his son and the expression in them hardened.

"Your report, Kendric," he said, "is not what I

hoped or expected. With one accord your Tutors say you could do better if you tried, and it is beyond my comprehension why you do not do so."

"I do, Papa," Prince Kendric said defiantly, "but if you ask my opinion the way we are taught is old-fashioned and, frankly, extremely dull."

This was such plain speaking that the Arch-Duchess drew in her breath and Zena looked at her brother nervously.

"It is a bad workman who complains of his tools," the Arch-Duke said sharply.

"If you had allowed me to go to University . . ." Kendric began.

This was an old argument and the Arch-Duke interrupted:

"You are to go into the Army. It is essential that when you take my place you should be able to command our troops, and God knows the discipline will be good for you!"

There was a pause and it was obvious that Prince Kendric was biting back the words he wanted to utter. As father and son glared at each other the Arch-Duchess interposed:

"Do continue and tell the children your plans, Leopold. That is what they have to hear."

Almost as if she called him to attention the Arch-Duke continued:

"Your mother and I have discussed the reports in detail and yours, Zena, are no better than Kendric's, especially where German is concerned."

"I find the grammar very difficult, Papa," the

Princess replied, "and Herr Waldshutz is, as Kendric says, so long-winded and so slow that it is difficult not to go to sleep."

"Very well, I take your point," the Arch-Duke said, "and that is why we have decided to send both you and Kendric to Ettengen."

"To Ettengen, Papa!" Zena exclaimed in astonishment.

"It is essential that Kendric's German should improve," the Arch-Duke said, "before he goes to Dusseldorf."

There was an audible gasp from Kendric before he asked, with his voice rising:

"Why should I be going to Düsseldorf and what for?"

"That is what I am about to tell you," the Arch-Duke said. "Your brother-in-law has suggested, and I think it is an excellent idea, that you should spend a year in the Barracks there and thus have the chance of joining in the intensive training which is given to the Officer Cadets of the Prussian Army."

"A year with those bloodthirsty warmongers!" Prince Kendric exclaimed. "I cannot imagine anything more like the terrors of hell!"

"It will be good for you, and you will do as you are told," the Arch-Duke replied.

"I refuse! I absolutely refuse!" Prince Kendric muttered, but besides the defiance, there was a note almost of despair in his voice.

"As for you, Zena," the Arch-Duke went on, turning again to his daughter, "as you two make such a fuss at being parted from each other, you will go with Kendric to Ettengen and try to improve your German, after which, when Kendric goes to Düsseldorf, your mother and I have planned your marriage."

If Kendric had been astonished it was now Zena's turn.

"Married, Papa?" the Princess questioned, and there was no mistaking the expression of horror in her eyes.

"You are eighteen, and we have been thinking for some time about finding you a suitable husband," the Arch-Duke said. "I personally hoped there would be a reigning Prince in one of our adjacent States, but unfortunately they are either married or too young."

Zena gave a little sigh of relief and her father continued:

"It was then your mother thought that it might be a good idea for you to marry one of her own countrymen. After all, I was very fortunate in having a relative of the Queen of England as my wife."

The Arch-Duchess inclined her head at the compliment. Then as if she could not forbear to join in she said:

"You must understand, Zena, that it would be impossible, as you are only a second daughter, for us to find a Royal Prince as your husband or, as I would have liked, a reigning Sovereign."

"But I have no wish to be married to . . . anybody, Mama!"

The Arch-Duchess frowned.

"Do not be so ridiculous!" she said sharply. "Of course you have to be married, and with Kendric away at Düsseldorf the sooner the better, as far as I am concerned. I know how tiresome you will be without him."

As this was true Zena looked across the table at her twin only to find he was scowling at a silver mustard-pot in front of him and obviously engrossed in his own troubles.

"I have written to my sister Margaret," the Arch-Duchess went on, "who is, as you are aware, a Lady of the Bedchamber to Queen Victoria and enjoys Her Majesty's confidence. We are in fact very fortunate and grateful to have her advice."

"And what is that, Mama?" Zena asked, feeling as if her lips were too dry for the words to pass through them.

"My sister Margaret replied that since there were no Royal Princes available at the moment of the right age, she had suggested to the Queen, who gave her approval, that you should marry an English Duke."

The Arch-Duchess paused, but as Zena did not speak, she continued:

"There are in fact two at the moment whose families on the maternal side have some connection with the Royal Family, and both my sister and the Queen thought that being the case that an alliance between one of them and us would be advantageous to both countries."

"But . . . I do not wish to marry an . . . Englishman, Mama."

"What possible objection can you have to the English?" the Arch-Duchess asked angrily.

It struck Zena that whatever she replied would inevitably entail being rude to her mother. She therefore merely looked down at her plate.

"I will ignore that exceedingly childish remark," the Arch-Duchess said scathingly.

"Get to the point, my dear," the Arch-Duke interposed. "We cannot stay here all day."

"That is just what I am trying to do, Leopold," his wife replied coldly, "but the children keep interrupting."

"They are quiet enough now," the Arch-Duke remarked.

"To get back to what I was saying," the Arch-Duchess continued without hurry, "my sister Margaret said there were two Dukes we might consider as your future husband, although she thought in fact that the Duke of Gatesford was too old, although he has recently become a widower."

The Duchess waited as if she expected Zena to ask his age, and as she did not do so, she went on:

"His Grace has turned sixty, and while he is of great importance and has a most commendable character, your father and I have decided that my sister is right and that he should not be approached."

"I could hardly marry a man who is older

than Papa!" Zena said.

"You will marry who we tell you to," the Arch-Duchess replied repressively, "and we have therefore chosen, though somewhat reluctantly, the Duke of Faverstone who is only thirty-three. His mother was a second cousin of the Queen and was also distantly related to Her Majesty's uncle, the Duke of Cambridge."

"There is nothing wrong with the fellow's antecedents," the Arch-Duke remarked.

"Of course what you say is true, Leopold," the Arch-Duchess agreed. "At the same time I would have wished Zena to marry an older man who would not only have controlled the regrettably frivolous side of her nature, but also given her a greater sense of responsibility towards the position into which she has been born."

"She will learn all that sooner or later," the Arch-Duke growled.

He was exceedingly fond of his second daughter and thought she resembled him more than any other of his children did. He was therefore always inclined to defend her against the criticism and fault-finding of her mother.

The Duchess favoured her oldest son, but her real affection was for her younger son who was not yet fourteen.

There was something about Prince Louis that made him appear more English than the rest of her children, and he was therefore automatically very close to the Arch-Duchess's heart.

She was a cold woman, brought up austerely

in England in a household where it was considered vulgar and ill-bred to show one's emotions.

When she had been married off, because of her Royal connections, to the Ruler of Wiedenstein, she had fallen in love with her handsome husband on sight, but found it impossible ever to express her feelings.

The Arch-Duke in those days had been a romantic Romeo who loved pretty women and who had indulged in a great many fiery love affairs before he was married.

He did not understand his wife but he treated her with respect and even grew to have some affection for her sterling qualities.

He would, however, have been astonished if he had known how wildly jealous she was of the women he favoured or how much she suffered from knowing that he did not admire her cold statuesque looks.

Nevertheless they had produced between them a family of outstandingly beautiful children.

It was, however, the Arch-Duchess thought, extremely unfortunate that her three daughters should take after their father in looks and in temperament, while her eldest son, Prince Kendric also leaned more towards Wiedenstein than the English side of his birthright.

She therefore hoped that her two younger children would be different and so far Prince Louis seemed more likely to fulfil her fondest hopes.

Zena was thinking over what her mother had

said and while she thought the Duke of Faver-stone sounded more hopeful than the other candidate, she had no wish to marry an Englishman.

She had never, even when she was small, found a soft spot in her mother's character to make her feel warm and cosseted.

In fact, the Arch-Duchess's continual scoldings, the severe punishments she had received as a child, and the way in which her opinions were always swept to one side, made her feel the whole English race was arrogant, dictatorial and heartless.

When she had thought about being married she had hoped, dreamed and prayed that she might marry a Frenchman.

The small Kingdom of Wiedenstein was situated West of Bavaria, with which one of its boundaries marched.

On the North there was the Province of Heidelburg belonging to Prussia, and on the West there was just a short frontier with the Alsace Region of France.

The majority of the population of Wiedenstein was of French origin who had intermarried with Bavarians.

Zena and her brother were therefore bilingual in French and German but their Tutor who was a Prussian continually found fault with the soft-spoken colloquial German of the Bavarians.

English was always spoken by the family in the Palace out of respect for the Arch-Duchess.

It was inevitable, as Zena had said when she

was out of hearing of her father, that the Wiedensteins should be a nation of mongrels, and moreover in their own family their father's mother had been half-Hungarian.

"Everybody knows," Kendric had once said to his sister, "that accounts for the wild streak in both of us."

"We have not had much chance of showing it," Zena replied resentfully.

"We shall have to wait until we are grown up," Kendric answered.

Now that he had left School and she was free of the School-Room except for visiting Tutors, they were to be separated and Zena's heart cried out at the idea, for she was sure that when she lost Kendric she would lose half of herself.

The family were at last allowed to leave the Breakfast-Room and Zena had to listen to Kendric's account of the horrors to which he would be subjected in a German Barracks.

"I have heard of the Cadets being ordered about like animals," he said. "When they have any free time they are forced to duel with each other, and the more scars they get on their faces, the prouder they are."

Zena gave a little cry of horror.

"Oh, Kendric, that must not happen to you!"

"It will," Kendric replied grimly.

He was an exceedingly handsome young man who enjoyed his good looks, and to Zena the idea of his being deliberately disfigured was terrifying.

17

They had rushed to their own private Sitting-Room as soon as they could get away from their parents, and now they looked at each other despairingly.

It was as if their whole world which had seemed safe and secure had collapsed and tumbled them into a slough of despond from which there was no escape.

"What shall we do?" Zena asked. "What can we do, Kendric? I cannot lose you for a whole year!"

"It is not only for a year," Kendric corrected, "but for life!"

Zena gave a cry.

"I shall have to marry that horrible Duke and it will be even worse than what poor Melanie has to endure with Georg."

The twins were silent, both thinking of the unhappiness of their older sister. She was married to the Crown Prince of Fürstenburg which was an allegedly independent State in the North of Germany, but was actually under the heel of Prussia.

Melanie had hated the Prince from the very moment she first saw him, but the marriage had gone ahead as arranged and when she occasionally came home she told the twins how unhappy she was.

"I loathe Georg," she had said over and over again. "He is pompous, obstinate and extremely stupid!"

"Oh, Melanie, I am sorry!" Zena cried.

"He listens to nothing anybody says except himself," Melanie went on, "with the result that everybody at Court is so deadly dull that I feel as if I am buried alive."

Her sister's words came back to Zena now, and she thought that was what would happen to her.

If all the English were like her mother, she would be suffocated by them.

She had actually met very few English people except for her mother's relations who came to stay from time to time.

The Arch-Duchess had been the youngest of a large family and her sisters and brothers had all married Royalty. They gave themselves, Zena thought, more airs and graces than any Wiedenstein ruler would think of doing.

The only time they were in the least human was when they were talking about horses, and what her father had said before they left the Breakfast-Room made Zena sure that the Duke of Faverstone would be exactly like them.

"Your mother suggested, Zena," he had said to his daughter, "that we invite the Duke of Faverstone here next month for the *Prix d'Or*."

This was the most important race-meeting of the year, and owners brought their horses from all over Europe to compete for the main prize.

Zena did not answer and her father had continued:

"Faverstone will thereby see us at our best and will meet the élite of the country. We will entertain for him in a manner which will make it quite clear he would have no grounds for thinking, because he is related to the Queen of England, that he can treat us condescendingly."

"You have no reason to imagine he will do that, Leopold," the Arch-Duchess had said defensively.

"I know the English," the Arch-Duke had replied, and Zena thought he had merely said aloud what she was thinking.

"What can we do to prevent these horrors from happening to us?" she now asked her brother.

Kendric did not reply and she went on:

"It is appalling that we are to be separated in addition to having to go to Ettengen and mug up that ghastly German."

"I hate that language too," Kendric said, "and from all the Baron tells me the Professor is even more boring than he is."

"You can be quite certain of that," Zena agreed. "After all, he must be a hundred and eighty, otherwise we would not have to go to him."

The Arch-Duke's last announcement had been that they were to leave in three days time for a small village where they were to stay with their Tutor, Professor Schwarz, because he was too old to come to them.

"You will be accompanied," their father had continued, "by Baron Kauflen and Countess Beronkasler, who will see that you two behave

20

yourselves and apply yourselves to your studies. Otherwise, when you return, I will be extremely angry!"

"Fancy having to stay for three weeks with those old bores!" Kendric said now.

"I feel like running away," Zena said gloomily. "The only difficulty is . . . where could we . . . run to?"

There was silence, then Kendric suddenly said:

"I have an idea!"

Zena looked at him apprehensively.

"If it is going to get us into more trouble with Mama, I do not think I could stand it!" she said. "You know what happened the last time you had one of your brainwaves."

She was however not speaking severely, but smiling.

The twins had always got into mischief ever since they were born and it was Kendric who with his vivid imagination thought out the outrageous pranks which inevitably brought retribution down on their heads.

But Zena would slavishly do whatever he wanted her to do simply because she loved him.

Kendric jumped up to walk across the room.

Their private Sitting-Room was very untidy simply because the servants had given up trying to create order out of chaos.

Kendric's guns, rackets, riding-whips, footballs and polo-sticks were all muddled up with Zena's paintbrushes and palettes, her embroi-

21

dery which she thought a boring pastime, but on which her mother insisted, and the books which she loved and which increased in number almost daily.

Books filled the shelves around the room, there were books on the table, on the chairs and on the floor.

There were also flowers which Zena had picked herself from the Palace garden and arranged with an artistry that was seldom shown in other parts of the Palace.

There were dolls she had loved as a child but which she now kept as ornaments and dressed them in beautiful gowns embroidered with jewels to brighten the severity of the panelled walls.

It suddenly struck Zena looking round the room that anyone seeing it for the first time would have a very clear insight into not only hers and Kendric's interests, but also their personalities and characters.

Quite suddenly Kendric gave a cry, jumped up and ran to the door. He opened it, looked outside, and shut it again.

"I am just making sure," he explained, "that there is nobody listening outside. I feel certain that on two or three occasions one of the maids or a footman has overheard our conversations, related them to Mama's lady's-maid, who in her turn wasted no time in passing on the information to Mama."

"So that is how Mama knew about your pretty

little dancer!" Zena said.

"There is no other possible way she could have known!" Kendric replied.

There had been an appalling row because the Arch-Duchess had learnt that Kendric had been out at night alone.

He had somehow evaded the sentries at the gate and gone to the Theatre where he had not only enjoyed night after night the performance of a very attractive Russian ballet dancer but had also taken her out to supper afterwards.

After the roof had nearly been taken off the Palace over his "outrageous behaviour", Kendric had decided that the only possible way his mother could have discovered his escapades was that he had extolled the dancer's charms and the fun they had together to Zena in the privacy of their Sitting-Room.

That was why now to make quite certain there was nobody listening he took the precaution of lowering his voice, and he sat down beside Zena before he began.

"Now listen," he said, "I have an idea and you must help me work out every detail."

"What is it?" Zena asked.

"You know where the Professor lives?"

"I know the direction on the map," Zena said.

"Well, to get there we have to change at the Junction of Hoyes."

Zena was now looking at her brother in a puzzled fashion.

He had a sudden light in his eyes which had

23

replaced the expression of dull despair, as if his plan was already exciting him, but at the same time she was afraid of what it might be.

"You know what happens at Hoyes," he went on.

"You tell me," Zena answered.

"Express trains from many parts of Europe stop there on their way to Paris."

The way Kendric spoke made Zena sit up sharply and look at him with startled eyes.

"What do you mean? What are you suggesting?" she asked.

"I am planning," Kendric said slowly, "how we can escape from our watch-dogs at Hoyes and spend a week of our tutorial in the gayest city in the world."

"You must be mad!" Zena exclaimed. "If we ran away from them they would come straight back and report to Papa, and he would have us arrested."

"I do not think so, for he would do nothing to cause a scandal," Kendric said. "At the same time, we have to be clever enough, Zena, to prevent those gloomy old vultures telling him anything for fear they will get into trouble."

There was a sparkle in Zena's blue eyes.

"Are you really saying, Kendric, that you think we can go to Paris instead of to that boring old Professor?"

"It is not what I *think* we can do," Kendric replied, "it is what I intend we shall do!"

"I think Papa and Mama will kill us!"

"Only if they find out."

"How are we going to prevent them? And supposing people recognise us?"

"Once we reach Paris nobody will recognise us, or know who we are," Kendric replied.

"You mean we will be disguised?"

"Of course we will! You do not suppose I am going to arrive as 'Crown Prince Kendric of Wiedenstein,' and have our Embassy preventing us from doing anything except look at Museums."

"But, Kendric, it is too dangerous, too outrageous!"

"God knows, I am entitled to do something outrageous if I am to spend a year clicking my heels and obeying orders at the double!" Kendric said bitterly.

"It is cruel of Papa to send you to such a place, and I am sure he is only being persuaded into it by our ghastly brother-in-law!"

"It is the sort of place that Georg would think enjoyable," Kendric said.

"But . . . can we really get to Paris?" Zena asked.

She knew that if once Kendric began a tirade against Georg whom they both disliked, it would depress them more than they were already.

Sometimes Zena would lie awake in tears when she thought of what her sister was suffering with such a man.

The thought of Georg made her remember that she was to marry an Englishman and because the idea was so horrifying she said quickly:

25

"Go on with your plan of how we can get there, how we can manage it, and who we shall say we are."

"We will escape from the old crows at Hoyes," Kendric said. "Once we are in the Express nobody will be able to stop us from reaching Paris. Of course they could telegraph a description of us down the line, but I think I can prevent them from doing that."

"How?" Zena asked.

"I will tell you that later," Kendric replied. "It is not yet quite clear in my mind."

"Then go on about when we reach Paris."

"From that moment Prince Kendric and Princess Marie-Thérèse will no longer exist."

"Then who shall we be?"

Kendric looked at her somewhat quizzically.

"It is going to be very restricting for me if I arrive in Paris with a sister who has to be looked after and chaperoned."

"It might be worse if I pretend to be your wife," Zena retorted.

"Exactly," he answered, "and that leaves only one alternative."

"What is that?"

"You must become my 'Chère Amie'. It will be rather like taking an apple to a Harvest Festival, but I could not be so unkind as to go to Paris without you."

Zena gave a cry.

"How could you even think of anything so selfish, so utterly disloyal and cruel? Of course

26

you must take me with you!"

Kendric put his hand on hers.

"We have always done everything together, and as this will be the most outrageous and our last escapade, even if we are discovered, it will have been worth it."

"Of course it will!" Zena said loyally.

"Very well," Kendric said, "and actually it will be a very good disguise."

"What will?"

"The part you will play as my lady-love."

Zena threw back her head and laughed.

"Oh, Kendric, do you think I dare? Think what Mama would say if she knew!"

"Let us pray that she never finds out!" Kendric said firmly. "But you do see that if you are thought to be a *demi-mondaine,* as a newly coined word expresses it, you will be able to come with me to all the places where ladies are not allowed to go?"

Zena clasped her hands together.

"That will be thrilling, only you will have to tell me how to behave."

She paused before she said provocatively:

"I am quite certain that is something you know all about!"

"Of course I do," Kendric boasted.

"And you also know where we should go in Paris?"

"I have a pretty good idea," he replied. "As you are aware, I have not been to Paris since I was grown-up and the last time was two years ago, but my friends at School, several of whom were older than me, talked of little else."

He smiled as if at the remembrance of what he had heard and went on:

"And Philippe whose father was in the Diplomatic Service, has told me all about the women who are under the protection of the Emperor, the Prince Napoleon and every important Statesman and aristocrat, and who charge astronomical sums for their services."

Zena looked puzzled.

"What services?" she asked.

Kendric realised he had been carried away by his enthusiasm and replied hastily:

"Because the gentlemen with whom they are — friends show them off to each other, they expect to be bedecked in jewels."

"You mean it is a sort of competition, like who has the best horses?" Zena asked.

"Exactly!" her brother replied. "And you will have to dress yourself up and of course use cosmetics, otherwise I shall lose a great deal of face when I produce you."

"That will not be difficult," Zena said, "for as you know Mama has always said that my looks are 'regrettably theatrical'!"

Kendric laughed.

"I have heard her say that often enough. It is the effect of your hair and your eyes, but there is nothing you can do about it."

"Nothing," Zena agreed, "but now perhaps the combination will come in useful."

Kendric looked at her as if he had never seen her before.

"You know, Zena," he said, "I think if you were not my sister I would be bowled over by you."

"Would you really, Kendric?" Zena asked with interest. "Well, I will certainly try not to shame you in Paris, and I have some new gowns that I think should be smart enough."

"You had better doll them up a bit." Kendric said. "From all I have heard the women who set the pace are 'dressed to kill'. Somebody was saying to Papa after dinner the other night that the Empress spends 1,500 francs on a gown."

"Good gracious!" Zena exclaimed. "I can hardly be expected to compete with that!"

"No, of course not," her brother replied, "but if we take enough money with us perhaps you will be able to buy one gown that will not look out of place, and at least you have some good jewellery."

"You mean what my grandmother left me?" Zena asked. "It is kept in the safe, but I expect I could get hold of it."

"I shall not appear to have been very generous unless you do," Kendric said.

He looked at his sister again. Then he said:

"You will be all right if you mascara your eyelashes and put on a bit of paint and powder. After all, not every man in Paris can have a million francs to throw away on a woman."

"Is that what they usually spend?" Zena asked in a low voice.

"I have heard of one woman called 'La Païva'," Kendric replied lowering his voice again, "who has millions of francs spent on her by every man she meets!"

"Why? Is she so beautiful?" Zena enquired.

It passed through Kendric's mind that as his sister was so innocent it was going to be difficult to answer her questions without embarrassing explanations which he felt it was not his business to make.

At the same time he knew, as Zena had said, he could not be so cruel as to leave her behind.

With his usual happy-go-lucky attitude he thought it would somehow work out all right in the long run.

If Zena guessed the reason for the notorious Courtesans' appearance and behaviour it would not eventually matter very much, while if he said as little as possible she would doubtless remain in happy ignorance of the reality of their behaviour.

Actually he was feeling rather ignorant himself.

He had had two very minor love-affairs, one of which was with the dancer before he had been strictly forbidden to see her again, and one which had been able to last much longer when he was at School.

His parents would have been horrified if he had realised that the older boys considered themselves men, and there were certainly young women from the town in which the School was situated to tell them they were.

But such affairs, Kendric knew, were very different from the methods by which the Courtesans who were the Queens of their profession ruled Paris.

The stories of their wild extravagance and the way they were fêted and acclaimed lost nothing in the telling.

Kendric had had an irresistible desire to visit Paris for the last year and he had suggested it again and again to his father. But the Arch-Duke had said:

"I would dearly like to take you there, my boy, but you know the fuss your mother would make if I suggested that we went for pleasure, and at the moment since politically we are somewhat at loggerheads with the French Government I cannot think of a really good excuse."

He had seen the disappointment on his son's face, and smiled understandingly.

"I will tell you what we will do, Kendric," he said. "Give it another year, and then when your mother will have no more jurisdiction over you we will get there somehow. I do not disguise the fact that I should enjoy it myself."

He gave a little sigh as he said:

"I often sit here wondering if 'La Castiglione' is still as beautiful as she is reported to be. I know that she is now the mistress of the Emperor."

31

"Was she a 'love' of yours, Papa?" Kendric asked.

He thought for a moment his father was not going to reply. Then he said:

"Very briefly, and although when she was young she was the loveliest thing I have ever seen she was actually somewhat boring."

He laughed before he added:

"But then *'les expertes ès Sciences galantes* are there to be looked at and loved, and why should we ask for more!"

"Why indeed, Papa?" Kendric had agreed.

'If we are caught,' he thought now, 'Papa will understand.'

But he knew neither his father nor his mother would ever understand or forgive him for taking Zena with him into what the Arch-Duchess considered a 'cesspool of wickedness'.

Kendric knew without Zena having to tell him how much she dreaded having to marry anybody, let alone an Englishman.

They were both of them deeply distressed about Melanie's unhappiness and the fact that the husband chosen for her was a man without a vestige of sensitivity or kindness.

From a social point of view it was a brilliant marriage, and as Fürstenburg was a far larger and more important country than Wiedenstein, Melanie would eventually be a Queen.

But as Zena had once said to her twin:

"Who in their senses would want to be a Queen except on a pack of cards? And if one was a man, one would rather be the Knave."

Kendric had laughed and agreed with his sister, but he thought now that just as no young man in his senses would want to go to the Barracks at Düsseldorf, so nobody as spirited and warm-hearted as Zena would wish to marry an Englishman.

"We both of us deserve a visit to Paris first," he told himself firmly.

And if his conscience pricked him he was determined not to listen to anything it said.

# Chapter Two

In the train which was carrying them to Hoyes, Zena was aware that her heart was beating nervously and she found it impossible to read the book which the Countess Bernkasler had bought for her edification on the journey.

It was only a two-hour ride from the Capital to Ettengen and the Arch-Duke had not bothered to provide his children with a Royal coach.

Instead a carriage was reserved on the train and they were seen into it by a Lord-in-waiting, the Station Master and a number of other railway officials.

They were in fact, travelling incognito. This was an excuse for the Arch-Duke not to send a military escort with them on the train or to have sentries posted outside the Professor's House in Ettengen.

As soon as they left the Capital, therefore, Kendric became the *Comte* de Castelnaud and Zena the *Comtesse*. It was actually one of the Arch-Duke's minor titles.

When the train left the capital Kendric had looked at his sister meaningfully and she knew their escape depended not only on her following his instructions to the letter, but also a great deal on chance.

If the Express to Paris was late, the slow train in which they were travelling might leave Hoyes before it, and they would be carried on to where the Professor was waiting to give them three weeks of unutterable boredom.

In the days before their departure, Kendric talked of nothing else when they were alone, and he was also managing, Zena knew, to see his French friend, Philippe, who he told her was a mine of information.

Both the Countess and the Baron were elderly and having settled themselves down comfortably in the carriage they made no attempt at conversation, but closed their eyes and apparently dozed off into unconsciousness.

Zena and Kendric knew they dare not assume that they were really asleep, and they therefore did not talk. But because they were twins they were each aware of what the other was thinking.

Finally when they had travelled for an hour and a quarter the train puffed slowly into Hoyes.

They had already stopped three times at wayside stations to pick up other passengers, mostly farmers and their wives or students. At the last of these stations Kendric had said:

"I must stretch my legs."

Baron Kauflen had opened his eyes.

"Do you wish me to accompany Your Royal Highness?"

"No, no, of course not," Kendric replied. "I

35

am going to walk very quickly to the end of the platform and back again. You just stay where you are, Baron."

The Baron had given a sigh of relief and Kendric hurried away.

Zena knew he had gone to arrange for their luggage to be taken from the Guard's Van at the end of the train and placed in the Paris Express.

The luggage had been another problem which on Kendric's instructions she had managed with what she thought was extreme cleverness.

"You can hardly be expected to take your best Ball-gowns and your more elaborate dresses to Ettengen," he said. "You must therefore have another trunk which you must pack yourself and I will tear off the label when we reach the station before Hoyes and tie on another one which I shall have in my pocket."

"Oh, Kendric!" Zena had exclaimed, "things become more and more complicated at every moment. Surely my maid will think it very strange if I pack a trunk myself?"

"You will just have to think of some excuse," Kendric said firmly. "Anyway, Maria is devoted to you, and if you swear her to secrecy I do not believe she will sneak to the other servants or, worst of all, to Mama."

Zena was certain this was true and she told Maria that she wished to take some of her more attractive gowns with her just in case she was asked to a dance.

"Please, Maria, do not say anything about it to

anybody," she begged, "because as I have told you, His Royal Highness and I are being sent to Ettengen to study, but three weeks is a very long time to look at nothing but books."

Maria had been sympathetic.

"My mother's always said, Your Royal Highness, that one's only young once, and I'll do nothing to spoil your fun."

"I trust you Maria."

To make sure she kept silent Zena gave her one of her gowns which she knew Maria had always admired, and the maid had promised to help her in every way she could.

In the end Maria had packed the extra trunk far more skilfully than Zena could have done, and also insisted that she took two hat-boxes one of which contained her more elaborate bonnets which she only wore on public occasions.

When Kendric came back to the carriage after his supposed walk he had winked at Zena and she knew he had been successful not only in changing the labels, but in tipping the Guard enough to ensure that the luggage would be transferred to the Paris Express.

There was, however, no sign of the fast train when their own train came to a standstill in the station.

A number of people alighted and Kendric opened the window to lean out, apparently watching them.

Zena began to grow afraid that all their plans would be circumvented at the last moment.

Then seeing Kendric's head turn she knew that he was suddenly alert and there was no need to tell her that the Express was in sight.

Porters hurried across the platform to where the train would wait for only a few minutes before it proceeded on to Paris.

Ostentatiously Kendric yawned.

"I am bored with having to wait about," he said to nobody in particular. "I think I will go to the bookstall and see if I can buy some more newspapers."

"Shall I do that for Your Royal Highness?" the Baron asked.

"No, I would rather choose them for myself," Kendric answered in an indifferent tone.

He opened the carriage door and stepped down on to the platform, leaving the door open.

This was the moment, Zena knew, when she had to be ready.

After a second she rose to her feet to stand as her brother had done at the window apparently watching the activity on the platform.

Then she saw Kendric beckon to her and she said to the Countess:

"His Royal Highness wants me, I will not be a moment."

As she spoke she put a letter she was holding in her hand down on the seat she had just vacated and jumped down on to the platform.

She heard the Countess expostulate as she ran to her brother's side. He took her hand and without pausing they ran to the Paris train.

The Porters were just slamming the doors of the carriages and the Guard had the whistle between his lips.

Kendric pulled open the door of a First Class carriage and pushed Zena into it.

The train was already moving as he jumped on the running board himself and a Porter shouted at him for leaving things so late and slammed the door shut behind them.

They threw themselves down on the carriage seats, for the moment too breathless to speak.

Then as the train gathered speed they realised they had done it — they had got away and there was nothing their attendants could immediately do about it.

The carriage they were in was empty and Zena guessed that while Kendric was waiting to signal to her he had chosen it with care.

Now he looked at her and burst out laughing.

"Tell me I am a genius!" he said. "Everything has gone like clockwork! The luggage is in, I saw the Guard carrying it himself, and here we are, embarking on an adventure that will enthrall our grandchildren when we tell them about it."

Zena laughed.

"I am not concerned with my grandchildren," she replied, "but with Papa and Mama."

"There is no need to worry," Kendric said soothingly. "When the Baron reads the letter I have written to him he will not dare to tell Papa. He will be too afraid of losing his job."

"What did you put in it?" Zena asked.

"I told him we have decided to stay with a friend of mine for one week before we start our lessons. I told him we should be completely safe and there is no need for him or the Countess to worry about us."

"They will do so all the same," Zena murmured.

"I pointed out," Kendric went on, as if she had not spoken, "that if they tell Papa he will undoubtedly vent his rage not only on us, but on them for not taking us safely to our destination as they had been told to do."

"Poor things," Zena said, "they did not have a chance!"

"Nevertheless, Papa will hardly consider that an excuse, and I know what Mama would say. So I am quite certain they will keep mum."

"I sincerely hope so," Zena said nervously.

"Even if they do return to the Palace and tell Papa they have lost us," Kendric continued, "he will have a job finding us in Paris. In fact it will be like looking for two needles in the proverbial haystack."

"All I want now," Zena said, "is for you to tell me who we are and what are our names."

As she spoke she opened her handbag and drew out a small pot.

"And I think," she added, "I should start altering my appearance right away."

"You might as well," Kendric agreed.

"Mama was surprised to see me wearing so smart a dress just to travel to Ettengen."

Zena gave a little laugh.

"She scolded me for my extravagance, and said that this dress and pelisse were intended to be worn when the Duke of Faverstone arrived."

She had started to speak lightly, but as she said the Englishman's name her expression altered.

"Forget him, anyway for the next week," Kendric said quickly. "Remember only that you are my *Chère Amie* and you do not have to marry anybody."

"How lucky those ladies are!" Zena said beneath her breath.

As she spoke she had turned round to look in the little mirror which was fixed above the seats and was undoing the ribbons of her bonnet which were tied beneath her chin.

She had done her hair a little more elaborately than usual with curls falling down the back in the very latest fashion.

Wiedenstein prided itself in not being far behind Paris, and because most of its citizens had French taste the dressmakers slavishly followed the latest fashions in the French Capital, while the *coiffeurs* were always ready to introduce a new style to their clients.

Because the hairdresser who had been in attendance on the Palace for nearly twenty years had died, his son who had taken over the business was determined that Princess Marie Thérèse should be a good advertisement for him.

The Arch-Duchess had protested at the way in

which he had dressed her daughter's hair because she considered its colour was flamboyant enough without it being arranged except in a ladylike manner.

But the Arch-Duke had supported his daughter when she had said:

"I have no wish to look a dowd, Mama, and I am sure you do not want your Court to be as dull and lifeless as poor Melanie's."

She knew as she spoke that even her father and mother had found their visits to the Palace of Fürstenburg extremely boring and the Arch-Duke in his usual outspoken way had replied:

"My God! If I thought we were going to be like that I think I would abdicate!"

The Arch-Duchess had looked disapproving at his language but had said nothing, and Zena's new hairstyle had been forgotten.

Now watching her Kendric thought that in her silk gown swept to the back in the new fashion with a bustle trimmed with pleats and frills she could easily pass for the *Chère Amie* she was pretending to be.

As if she knew what he was thinking she turned round and he saw that she had applied a red salve to her lips and also powdered her already pearly white skin.

"How do I look?" she asked.

"Sensational!" Kendric replied. "In fact you not only look the part, but extraordinarily pretty!"

"Thank you!" Zena said. "When we reach

Paris I will blacken my eye-lashes, but I cannot do it in the train because the mascara might run into my eyes and make them smart."

She sat down opposite him and went on:

"Now tell me where we are going and what we are going to do."

"First of all," Kendric said dramatically, "let me introduce you to the *Vicomte* de Villerny."

Zena stared at him.

"But . . . he is a real . . . person!"

"Yes, I know," Kendric agreed, "and that is why it is clever of me to impersonate him."

"I know that the present *Vicomte* is somewhere out in the East," Zena said, "but suppose somebody knows what he looks like?"

"I think that is unlikely," Kendric replied, "and you know as well as I do the French are terrible snobs and sleep with the *Almanach de Gotha* under their pillows. If I had given a false name as I first intended, I might have been quickly exposed as an importer."

"I see your point," Zena replied.

The late *Vicomte* de Villerny had been a friend of their father's.

He was a distinguished man in his own field who had spent his life collecting shells of every sort and description, and writing books about them which were only read by conchologists.

Because his collection was world famous the children from the Palace were allowed frequently to visit him to see his latest acquisitions.

What they enjoyed more than the shells was

43

the fact that the *Vicomte* was also a gourmet who had given them delicious *patisseries* to eat and also insisted, even when they were very young, that they should drink a glass of wine with him.

When the *Vicomte* had died two years ago Zena had been genuinely sorry.

His son had inherited the title and of course, his collection of shells, but he preferred to live in the East where he had strange interests that were spoken about in Wiedenstein only in lowered voices.

Now she thought about it, Zena realised that Kendric was right in assuming a title that would not be questioned, and they were very unlikely to meet anybody who knew the present *Vicomte*.

"And who am I?" Zena asked now.

"You of course, are of no particular consequence," Kendric replied. "Although doubtless there will be a large number of men who will look at you, and look again."

He saw the smile on his sister's red lips and added quickly:

"Now you are to behave yourself, Zena! You know as well as I do that I have no right whatever to involve you in this escapade, and if you get into any trouble in the process God knows what will happen to me if Papa hears about it!"

"Why should I get into trouble?" Zena asked. "And of course I will behave myself properly! All I want to do is to see Paris and have some fun."

It crossed Kendric's mind that was the last thing she should be wanting in Paris of all places, but it was far too late to have regrets, and as he had said before, he could not have been so cruel as to leave his twin sister behind and enjoy himself on his own.

"I have been thinking of a name for you," he said, "and it ought to sound theatrical."

"Then I can keep my Christian name, at any rate," Zena said.

"Of course! Zena is very appropriate, and I could not risk your not answering when I speak to you."

"No, of course not," she agreed, "and what is my other name to be?"

"I thought of Beauchamp," Kendric replied.

Zena put her head on one side as she considered it.

"Fair field," she said. "It sounds rather engaging, but 'Bellefleur' would be even better."

"Of course! You are right!" Kendric agreed.

Zena chuckled before she said in French.

"*Mademoiselle* Zena Bellefleur at your service, *Monsieur!*"

She looked so pretty as she spoke that once again her brother felt apprehensive about what her impact would be on Paris.

Then he remembered it was a City where lived some of the most beautiful as well as the most notorious and outrageous women in Europe, and he told himself that among them Zena would pass unnoticed.

Because the Express was so fast it was only a two-hour journey from Hoyes to Paris, and as they came into the huge arched station Zena felt as if she was stepping into a new world, and she had never known such excitement before in her whole life.

They collected their luggage which was clearly marked: *THE PROPERTY OF THE VICOMTE DE VILLERNY* a porter loaded it on to a *voiture*.

As it set out over the cobbled streets Zena saw the tall grey houses with their wooden shutters, the Cafés in the Boulevards with the customers sitting outside on the pavement and felt as if the curtain was rising on an enthralling drama.

She found that her resourceful brother had already obtained accommodation for them.

"Philippe has a friend," he said, "who has a very comfortable apartment in the Rue St. Honoré. He is in Italy at the moment, and he told Philippe that any time he wished to go to Paris he could use his apartment."

"So he has actually offered it to us?" Zena asked.

"He has not only done that, but he has written to the caretaker to say that we are his guests, and everything is to be done for our comfort."

"How kind!" Zena cried. "It is very lucky you are such friends with him."

"I have often thought such a friendship might come in useful one day," Kendric confessed.

"We must certainly do something for him when we get home," Zena said.

She saw by the expression on her twin's face that he was thinking it would be over a year before he was able to entertain his friends or in any way recompense Philippe.

Because she had no wish to depress him Zena quickly changed the subject, pointing out the new Opera House which had not been finished when she had last been to Paris. Soon they were passing down the Rue de la Paix where all the important dressmakers had their Salons, including the famous Frederick Worth.

"That is where I want to buy a gown!" she said in a rapt voice.

"We will have to see what our expenses are first," Kendric said in a practical tone. "I have brought a lot of money with me but I know Paris is very expensive."

"At least we will not have to pay rent," Zena reminded him.

"No, but if we are going to enjoy ourselves we must entertain. Philippe has already written to some of his friends."

"He has not told them who we are?" Zena asked in horror.

"No, of course not!" Kendric said. "He merely said that I am the *Vicomte* de Villerny who lives in Wiedenstein and who is visiting Paris with a very lovely lady-friend."

Zena laughed.

"Oh, Kendric, you are wonderful! Nobody else could have planned anything so clever, or indeed so thrilling."

"That remains to be seen," Kendric said cautiously, but Zena saw that his eyes were shining.

The apartment was charming and was on the first floor of a large house at what Kendric said was 'the right end' of the Rue St. Honoré.

There was a large Sitting-Room, three bedrooms and to Zena's surprise a small kitchen.

"Why should the owner want a kitchen?" she asked. "Surely he would go out for his meals?"

"I expect he thinks sometimes it is more convenient to dine at home," Kendric answered, "and if the Caretaker is not prepared to cook for him, I am quite certain he would have a delightful *Chère Amie* who would be only too willing to oblige."

His eyes were twinkling as he spoke and Zena replied:

"You know as well as I do that I am a good cook, but I have no intention of cooking while we are in Paris! I want to visit all the Restaurants, if for no other reason because Mama says Royalty can never be seen in one!"

"You shall eat in all the most famous of them," Kendric promised. "I have a list."

"Then what are we waiting for?" Zena asked.

"For you to change your clothes," Kendric replied, "and there is no hurry. Nobody eats early in Paris, so you can forget your Provincial ways."

Zena made a grimace at him and went to the bedroom she had chosen for herself which was the largest and most attractive, where she found a young girl who she assumed was the caretaker's daughter unpacking her trunk.

48

"*M'mselle*'s gowns are very beautiful!" the girl said. "Are you going to the Artists' Ball?"

"Is it taking place tonight?" Zena enquired.

"*Oui, oui, M'mselle* and all Paris enjoys the gayest and most noisy Ball of the year. Everybody will be there, except perhaps the Empress who does not approve."

She paused to note that Zena was listening intently and went on:

"The Emperor is sure to attend. He enjoys seeing the pretty women who make each Ball more successful than the last."

Zena ran from the bedroom and across the Sitting-Room.

"Kendric!" she cried as she opened her brother's bedroom door. "Did you know that the Artists' Ball is taking place tonight? Please, let us go!"

"Of course we are going," Kendric replied. "I have not told you because I wanted it to be a surprise."

Zena looked at her twin who had just taken off his coat and tie. Then she flung her arms around his neck.

"Oh, Kendric, you are wonderful!" she said. "Who could have a more fabulous brother than you?"

Kendric smiled. Then he saw that the door was open and frowned.

"Hush," he said. "Have you forgotten I am not your brother? Even when we are here by ourselves we must be careful."

"I am sorry. It was stupid of me."

Zena spoke in a contrite tone.

"I do not suppose any harm has been done," Kendric said, "but do be on your guard. We must not arouse the slightest suspicion. Looking at you, I am quite certain a number of men will be very curious."

Zena kissed his cheek as she said:

"And as you are so handsome I am equally certain a large number of women will be curious about you."

"That is the sort of thing I expect to hear," Kendric said complacently.

"You are abominably conceited," Zena teased.

Then because she was in a hurry to get ready she went back to her own room.

As Kendric had said, there was no hurry, but by the time Zena had unpacked, had a bath, arranged her hair and made up her face in what seemed to her to be a very lurid fashion nearly three hours had passed.

She put on a gown which the Arch-Duchess had complained when she bought it was far too elaborate for a young girl.

It was in fact a copy of one of Mr. Worth's creations which the dressmaker in Wiedenstein had seen when she was in Paris and she had actually brought back the same material which Mr. Worth had used.

It was of blue shot with silver, which accentuated the red-gold of Zena's hair and made her blue eyes seem even larger and more brilliant than usual.

It was not surprising that she should have blue eyes considering that her father's eyes were blue and so were her mother's.

But Zena's were the colour of the gentians she had seen growing in the mountains when they had visited Switzerland and the combination of them with her white skin and her hair was positively sensational or, as the Arch-Duchess had said, 'regrettably theatrical'.

Zena had mascaraed her eyelashes to make them appear even longer than they were already, and reddened her lips.

Having done so she felt as if the Princess Marie-Thérèse had really ceased to exist and that she really was now a *demi-mondaine* a word she was sure would never soil her mother's lips.

She was still not certain why the *demi-mondaines* of Paris were considered so outrageous.

She supposed they were like actresses, remembering her mother had always said firmly that no decent woman would parade herself in public so that anybody could pay to watch her.

When she and Kendric entered the *Café Anglais* which her brother told her was the most fashionable and the most acclaimed Restaurant in all Paris, Zena felt as if she stepped on a stage.

It was very large which she had not expected, and she gathered there were a number of different rooms in it though she did not quite understand what that involved.

*Le Grand Seize* in which they were dining and which was downstairs was not full when they had entered but now began to fill up minute by minute until there was not an empty table in the whole place.

It was then that Zena was aware why Kendric had told her she must doll herself up and try to look her best.

Never had she imagined that women could be so fantastically gowned, or bedecked with so many jewels.

She found herself staring at them one after another as they came sweeping in from the *Vestibule*, their bustles moving behind them like the wake of a ship at sea.

Their hair fell in long ringlets behind their swan-like necks, and their bare chests and arms literally blazed with gems.

Kendric had ordered some of the specialities that were more delicious than any food Zena had ever tasted before, but it was difficult to appreciate such cuisine when all she could do was stare around her at the other diners.

"I wish we knew who all these people are," she said to Kendric.

"We will soon be told," he replied. "I found quite a number of invitations waiting for me at the apartment, and Philippe's friends seem glad to entertain us to luncheon, dinner, and of course, supper."

The way he said the last word made Zena look at him enquiringly.

"Is there something special about supper?" she asked.

"Of course," Kendric replied. "That is when we shall see the bright lights of Paris and visit the places where no 'nice girls' would go."

"It sounds thrilling," Zena said, "but tonight we are going to the Ball."

"We are joining some of Philippe's friends in a box," Kendric said, "but I warn you it may be rowdy, so do not be surprised."

It was so exciting that Zena could not make up her mind whether to stay on at the *Café Anglais* where there was so much to see, or whether they should hurry to the Ball.

Finally, when she felt it was growing late, although Kendric had laughed at her for thinking so, they set off for the Ball, and she thought that nobody could be more fortunate than she was, and that whatever happened in the future with the dull and doubtless incredibly boring Duke, she would have this to remember.

When they reached the Artists' Ball the lights, the music and the wild dancing of hundreds of guests were dazzling.

They were shown up to the second tier of boxes and Kendric soon found the box where they were to meet Philippe's friends.

They were obviously expecting him and he was greeted with an exuberance which Zena thought was rather overdone until she realised that the gentlemen in the box had all imbibed a great deal from the innumerable bottles of champagne stacked on a table just inside the door.

"Come in! Come in!" they shouted. "Philippe has asked us to look after you and that is what we are delighted to do."

Kendric shook them by the hand and was introduced to four young women who were with them. Then he introduced Zena.

She thought the women were over-painted and under-dressed. In fact she felt embarrassed at the lowness of their décolletage and the way when they were sitting they exposed their silk-stockinged legs.

Two of them on being introduced to Kendric kissed him effusively and when he had sat down one of them put her arm around his neck.

"You are very handsome, *mon cher*," Zena heard her say to him, "and I adore handsome men!"

She thought this was a strange way to behave, then told herself she must not be critical. This was the world she wanted to see, and whatever happened she must not appear embarrassed.

One of the gentlemen put a glass of champagne into her hand, then filled up everybody else's glass to the brim.

Down below them on the dance-floor Zena could see that a lot of the dancers were wearing fancy-dress and she guessed those were the students who would later in the evening produce tableaux and floats which they had constructed in the different Art Centres to which they belonged.

She had often read about this Ball in newspapers and magazines but although she had tried to visualise it, she found now that her imagination had fallen far short of the reality.

It was certainly very gay and as the Band played louder and faster and everybody swung round and round the floor in a waltz Zena felt almost dizzy as she watched.

One of their hosts, whose name Zena gathered was Paul although she had no idea what else he was called, said he wanted to dance and his friends agreed that they should go down below and join in the general *mêlée* on the dance-floor.

Kendric would have stayed behind but the lady who had already attached herself to him pouted provocatively and said she had every intention of dancing with him.

"I want your arms around me," she said, "and what could be a better excuse?"

"I assure you I do not need one," Zena heard her brother say.

They disappeared together from the box with the rest of the party leaving Zena alone with a young man who she realised was looking ill.

"Are you all right?" she asked as he sat down gingerly on the edge of a chair.

"I — will be all right," he answered slurring his words. "I — will go and get — some fresh air. It is too — hot in here."

He went from the box to leave her alone.

Zena was quite content to sit leaning over the edge of it so that she could watch without interruption the dancers down below. She could see

55

Kendric with both his partner's arms round his neck moving amongst the throng.

There were men dressed in ancient armour, or in nothing but an animal's skin, women in indecently transparent Grecian robes, an innumerable number of Pierrots and some very dubious Nuns.

It was all fascinating and she did not want to miss anything, even the scuffles that seemed to break out in various parts of the dance-floor when a man wished to dance with a woman who was dancing with another man who had no intention of relinquishing her.

One man who was more importunate than the rest received a blow on the chin which sent him sprawling on the polished floor and Zena gave a little chuckle to herself.

Then a voice beside her said:

"I see you are amused, *Mademoiselle*, and I am not surprised. I always think there is no spectacle as extraordinary as this."

Zena turned her head in surprise and realised that she had been spoken to by a gentleman in the box next to the one in which she was sitting.

There was only a thin partition between them and the red velvet ledges of their box formed one piece.

The gentleman in question was dark and from where she was sitting she felt because he was so broad-shouldered that he must be tall. He was also extremely handsome, but in a different way from her brother or her father.

He had spoken to her in French, but he looked different from the three young men who were Philippe's friends.

She thought it was because he was older and more distinguished-looking.

Realising he was waiting for an answer to his remark she said:

"This is the first time I have seen the Ball, so I find it fascinating."

"And is it also your first visit to Paris?"

She was just about to reply that she had not been there for many years when she thought it a strange question to ask.

After all, as she spoke French, why should he think she was anything but French?

Then she remembered that Kendric had said:

"It is always wise when you are in disguise to tell the truth as near as it is possible to do so."

"What do you mean by that?" Zena had questioned.

"If you are asked, you must say you have a French friend, but that you yourself come from Wiedenstein."

Zena had looked at him apprehensively.

"Why should I do that? Would it not be dangerous?"

"You do not look French," Kendric had said simply, "having far too much of Papa in you. At the same time you do not look Bavarian either, and after all there are a lot of women, one way or another, in Wiedenstein."

Zena laughed.

"Yes, of course," she had said, "I am just nervous of being denounced as an impostor, and I would much prefer to say I am from Wiedenstein."

"On that at least we agree," Kendric had replied, and they had both laughed.

Zena now realised there had been quite a considerable pause before she said:

"I feel I should be insulted that you think I do not look smart enough to be French!"

The gentleman smiled.

"I assure you, I have no thought of insulting you. In fact if you are looking for compliments, may I tell you you are very lovely, the loveliest woman here this evening."

"Thank you," Zena replied.

She told herself she must not look embarrassed but behave as if she received such compliments every day of her life.

"Let me continue by saying," the gentleman went on, "that your hair is the most unusual and ravishing colour I could possibly imagine. How can you be so original in the City of Originality?"

Zena laughed.

"I am not certain that is not another insult in that you are suggesting that I have created the colour of my hair."

"No, I know that would be impossible," the gentleman said. "Only a great artist could have done that, and who could be greater than God."

Zena looked at him wide-eyed.

"I adore your hair and also your straight little

nose and your incredibly beautiful blue eyes," the gentleman continued.

Quickly Zena remembered that as a *Chère Amie* she could not expect men to treat her with the respect and formality she had always received in the past.

Then when she looked into the dark eyes of the man to whom she was talking, she suddenly felt shy in a way she could not understand. She wanted to go away from him, and yet at the same time she wanted to stay.

"Shall we introduce ourselves?" the gentleman asked, "and perhaps to do so it would be more convenient if instead of talking with this barrier between us either I join you, or you join me."

Zena found his invitation somewhat startling. At the same time she thought it was a common-sense suggestion that she should not query.

After all, she had learned that the Artists' Ball was a place of licence, gaiety and good comradeship, and without a chaperon there was nobody to introduce her to this stranger.

"Perhaps," she said after a moment, "you should come into . . . this box, although my friend and I are only . . . guests and I have no . . . authority to . . . invite anybody else to join us."

"Then as I am alone in my box and it belongs exclusively to me," the gentleman answered, "may I suggest we should be more comfortable and less overcrowded here."

This seemed even more sensible, Zena

thought, and she was also aware that if the young man who felt ill returned she might have to talk to him or worse still to dance with him.

She was not so foolish as not to realise that he was ill because he had drunk far too much, and she had no wish to see any more of him.

"When your friend returns," the gentleman said, "it will be quite easy for you to see him over the partition, and he will not have to look far to find you."

"Yes, of course."

Zena rose from the chair in which she was sitting and moved towards the door of the box, having to negotiate not only some chairs to do so, but also a number of empty champagne bottles which had been thrown down on the floor.

Before she reached the door it opened and the gentleman from the next box was standing there.

She had been right, she thought, in thinking that he was tall and broad-shouldered and his eyes seeming darker than they had before looked at her in a way which she felt was slightly embarrassing.

At the same time, because it was undoubtedly a look of admiration she could not help feeling pleased.

It was only a few steps to the next box and as Zena went into it, because it was empty and tidy, it seemed infinitely preferable to the confusion she had just left behind.

The gentleman held an armchair for her to seat herself and she thought it was tactful of him to offer her the one in which he had been sitting and which was next to the partition which divided the boxes.

"Thank you," she said.

He pulled up a chair next to hers to say:

"Now tell me about yourself. I was feeling lonely and a little bored until I saw you, but now my evening is beginning to sparkle and I can feel the enchantment of Offenbach's music, which was missing before."

"I heard somebody say that it typified the spirit of Paris."

"I would say that so do you, except that I am convinced you are not French even though your accent is perfect."

Zena thought with a little smile that this, if nothing else, would please her father who was always so insistent that she should speak with a Parisian accent.

"Are you prepared to guess to which country I belong?" she asked.

The gentleman shook his head.

"No, because I have been trying to puzzle it out for myself ever since I saw you, and have failed dismally to find an answer."

"Perhaps I should leave you guessing," Zena said. "A puzzle is no longer interesting once one has finished it."

She thought as she spoke that it was a rather clever remark, but her companion leaned forward in his seat to say:

"This puzzle will not be finished when you tell

me where you were born. There is so much more I want to know; so much about you I find intriguing and, if I am honest, very exciting."

There was a note in his voice which again made her feel shy, and she told herself this was exactly the way she thought gentlemen would talk to the beautiful ladies she had heard about and whom she had seen tonight at the *Café Anglais*.

It was as if she was taking part in a performance on the stage, and she thought she would be very naïve and gauche if she missed her lines and behaved like an inexperienced and rather stupid schoolgirl.

"I think, as you spoke to me first, *Monsieur*," she said, "you should introduce yourself, as there is nobody to do it for you."

"Very well," he replied. "My name is Jean, and if I am to present myself formally, I am the *Comte* de Graumont."

"I am delighted to meet you, *Monsieur*," Zena said formally, "and I am Zena Bellefleur."

"*Enchante, Mademoiselle,* and what name could be more appropriate?" the *Comte* said.

He took her hand in his as he spoke and lifted it to his lips.

She had taken off her gloves as she was watching the dancers and when he kissed her hand she thought he would do it perfunctorily in the manner in which gentlemen bowed over her mother's and occasionally hers.

Instead the *Comte* actually kissed her skin and

she thought this a strange thing to do. At the same time, it was a rather exciting one.

Because she felt a little embarrassed she took her hand away from him and looked again at the dancers below them.

"Well, I am waiting," he said after a moment.

"For what?" she asked.

"For you to tell me where you come from, unless of course you have stepped down from Venus, or one of those other planets which I suspect are inhabited by goddesses as lovely as you."

Zena chuckled.

"I wish I could answer truthfully that I have just flown here on wings from the Milky Way. It would sound so much more alluring than coming from a mere European State."

"Whichever one it may be, it is exceptional if it is yours," the *Comte* said.

Once again Zena felt they were speaking the lines of the leading characters in a play.

They had their own Theatre in the Palace and, although the Arch-Duchess arranged that plays produced there were all classical dramas and anything that was not exceedingly proper was forbidden Zena still found the world of imagination behind the footlights a joy of which she never tired.

"Why are you smiling?" the *Comte* asked.

Zena told him the truth.

"I was thinking we are behaving as if we were performing a drama on the stage," she said, "and tonight because it is so exciting to be here, I feel as if I am a leading lady."

"Of course and a very beautiful one," the *Comte* said, "and I am very honoured that I should be playing opposite you or, should I say, with you."

Again there was a note in his voice that made Zena feel he was being intimate. Perhaps it was also the expression in his eyes, or that as he talked to her he seemed to be very close.

Finally, because it seemed stupid to prevaricate, she said:

"I come from Wiedenstein."

The *Comte* raised his eyebrows.

"Are you sure?"

"Of course I am sure. I must know where I belong."

"I am only surprised," he said, "because I thought that the Citizens of Wiedenstein would be very French. Frenchwomen are usually dark and somewhat sallow-skinned and although they are exceedingly vivacious and entertaining, they do not look like you."

"Not everybody in Wiedenstein looks like me," Zena smiled.

"I can well believe that," the *Comte* replied, "otherwise every man I know would be visiting Wiedenstein and the place would be overrun with eager Don Juans."

Zena laughed.

"What a lovely idea!"

"But I am afraid," the *Comte* went on, "you are unique, in which case although my whole idea of Wiedenstein has changed I cannot expect there to be thousands of Wiedenstein women looking like you."

His voice dropped, then became deeper as he said:

"As a thousand men or more must have told you already you are very, very lovely!"

The compliment took Zena by surprise, and because the way the *Comte* spoke seemed to vibrate through her she forgot for a moment who she was meant to be.

She looked into his eyes, then looked quickly away again.

"I do not . . . think," she said in a very small voice, "that you should . . . speak to me . . . like . . . that."

"Why not, when it is true?" he asked.

She did not answer him and after a moment he said:

"What you are really saying is that your friend with whom you came here would resent it and perhaps call me out."

"No!" Zena said quickly. "Of course he would not do that!"

"What I do not understand" the *Comte* went on, "is why he has left you alone. He must realise that if a man leaves treasure of great value unguarded he runs the risk of somebody stealing it from him."

Zena smiled.

"I do not think Kendric will worry about that, although I like to think I am a treasure of great value."

"There are so many other ways in which I could describe you," the *Comte* said, "but this is not a place in which I find it easy to do so."

As he spoke there was a sudden noise of voices and laughter in the box beside Zena and she looked over the partition to see that Kendric had come back with the girl with whom he had been dancing.

There were also the other gentlemen accompanied by women, and several men whom she had not seen before.

They were all intent on pouring out the champagne, and as she looked at them Kendric saw her in the corner of the other box and came towards her.

"Are you all right, Zena?" he asked.

"Yes, of course," Zena replied, "shall I come back?"

As if Kendric suddenly realised that she was not where he had left her he looked surprised, but before he could speak the *Comte* said:

"May I introduce myself? I am Jean de Graumont, and I invited *Mademoiselle* to join me as she was alone."

Kendric looked slightly shame-faced as he said to Zena:

"I thought there was somebody with you."

"There was," she agreed, "but he felt ill and went to get some fresh air."

"I thought I could take good care of *Mademoiselle* in your absence," the *Comte* said.

"That was very kind of you," Kendric replied.

"My name is de Villerny."

The *Comte* gave an exclamation.

"Do you mean the *Vicomte?* I heard that your father was dead."

"You knew him?" Kendric asked and Zena knew he was nervous.

"My father was extremely interested in shells," the *Comte* replied, "and he talked so much of the de Villerny collection that I almost feel as if I have seen it, though actually I have never been to Wiedenstein."

"Then I hope one day I may show it to you," Kendric answered and Zena thought how clever he was to speak so calmly.

"Thank you," the *Comte* said. "Perhaps one day I shall have the opportunity of accepting your invitation."

There was a pause. Then Kendric said as if he felt he ought to do so:

"Would you like to dance with me, Zena?"

"I think really I would rather watch from here," she replied. "It looks a little rough down there."

"It is," Kendric said ruefully.

He was just about to say more when the girl with whom he had been dancing came to his side and put her arms around him.

"You're neglecting me," she said, "and I think it's unkind of you. Get me a glass of champagne, then we must watch the Show which is just starting, after which we can go on somewhere else."

"No, I cannot do that," Kendric replied, "I have my friend with me."

"Then you'll have to bring her too, although three is a crowd," the woman said.

Kendric looked uncomfortable and the *Comte*, almost without a pause as if he came in on clue, said:

"Perhaps you would permit me as I am alone to make up the party."

Before Kendric could speak the girl who by now had her arm round his neck said:

"That's perfect! You come along, then we can all enjoy ourselves. I want to dance where it is not so crowded and with you, *mon cher*."

She kissed Kendric's cheek holding on to him in a way which made it impossible for the moment for him to release himself.

Zena realised she was staring, and because she had no wish to embarrass her brother she looked away.

She realised that the *Comte* was watching her and because there was an expression in his eyes which she also found embarrassing she deliberately looked over the edge of the box down at the dance-floor.

"The Show is going to start," she said, and knew that despite everything that was strange and made her feel shy it was very exciting.

At the same time it flashed through her mind that if her mother knew what she was doing the Arch-Duchess would undoubtedly have a heart attack.

# Chapter Three

'It must be very late, or rather very early in the morning,' Zena thought to herself.

Strangely enough she was not tired, but still excited and exhilarated by the whole evening.

The Show which the students put on at the Ball had taken a long time, but had been extremely amusing.

They brought in strange creations which they had made in their various Studios and when a prehistoric animal collapsed with dozens of students on top of it, everybody in the Ball-Room screamed and shouted their applause and Zena had found it very funny.

She was laughing at the chaos on the floor below when she realised that the *Comte* was watching her rather than the spectacle.

"Do look!" she said. "You have never seen such a mess!"

"I would rather look at you," he said in a low voice, and she hoped nobody had overheard him.

Actually there was no danger of that for the party which had returned to the box had not only increased in number but the women who joined it had drunk as much as the men and were very noisy about it.

Kendric did not seem surprised to find her with the *Comte* instead of the ill young man who had not returned at all and, as he was completely engrossed with Nanette, as Zena found the effusive young woman was called, she was extremely grateful that she had somebody to talk to.

Because she thought it was right when Kendric returned she had moved back into the box with his friends but she soon began to regret she had done so.

Everybody was jostling and trying to get to the front of the box to watch what was happening on the dance-floor, but in doing so they seemed at times in danger of falling over the edge, and Zena looked at them apprehensively.

She was glad when Kendric decided they should leave, but although she expected them to be a party of four as he had originally said, by the time they reached the *Chat Noir* in Montmartre the party had an addition of several strangers who were friends of Philippe's friends.

The *Chat Noir* was interesting but very noisy and they did not stay long since they found it was too crowded to dance.

The next place they went to had more room for dancing and there were women who appeared to behave in quite an outrageous fashion, dancing alone and showing an unseemly amount of leg and frilly petticoats.

"I have a feeling," the *Comte* said, "that you

are shocked by what you are seeing."

Zena was just about to say that was true when she remembered that as a *Chère Amie* and a *demi-mondaine* she should accept such behaviour.

"No, of course not," she said, "but it is very noisy here."

The *Comte* had suggested they should go elsewhere and whether it was because she wished it or that several men asked her to dance, Zena could not decide.

She had no wish to dance with any of the rest of the party because they were not only unsteady on their feet, but they shouted to each other on the dance-floor or tried to change partners with their friends, often when such an overture was unwelcome.

When one man asked her to dance and she refused, he had insisted, and the *Comte* had said:

"*Mademoiselle* is my partner," in a meaningful manner.

"Pardon," the man said immediately, "I did not realise she was your *petite poulé*."

He walked away and Zena tried to remember what *petite poulé* meant.

It was not a phrase that had entered her vocabulary so far.

It was obviously effective, for after that the men in the party left her alone and she noticed they danced with other women in the room.

When finally they left this place Zena saw

with surprise that Kendric was no longer with Nanette, but with another much more attractive French girl whose name was Yvonne.

He obviously found her very alluring and as they talked to each other in low, intimate whispers she realised that Kendric was holding Yvonne's hand.

This time, perhaps on the *Comte*'s suggestion, they went to a dance-hall in the *Champs Élysées* where the Band was playing a spirited Polka in a garden and the dancers were very mixed.

There were not only gentlemen in evening-dress like the *Comte* and their new friends, but there were also men in velvet coats and flowing ties who looked like artists, clerks in neat suits, and pretty *midinettes* in flower-decorated hats and with full skirts that swung round and round as they danced.

It was all very gay and the music was infectious. For the first time in the evening the *Comte* said to Zena:

"Shall we dance?"

She was aware that he had not asked her before because everywhere else they had been was so overcrowded that she felt it would be a case of barging around the room.

Now as she smiled her acceptance he drew her on to the floor and the Polka having come to an end the Band started to play one of Offenbach's dreamy romantic Waltzes.

Zena knew she could dance well, but dancing in the Palace Ballroom with Courtiers whose duty it was to partner her was very different from dancing with the *Comte.*

When he put his arm around her waist she thought he held her rather too closely and proprietorially, but again she told herself she must not complain.

As they started to move she realised that he danced extremely well and was easy to follow.

They danced without speaking, and Zena thought that the stars overhead and the glow of the gaslamps made the dance-hall the enchanted Paris she had wanted to find.

"I must enjoy every moment of it," she told herself, "so that I can remember it when everything is stiff, formal and pompous either at home or in England."

She gave an involuntary shiver as she thought of what she would find in that cold repressed country, and the *Comte* asked:

"What is troubling you? I want you to be happy this evening."

"I am happy."

"But just now you were thinking about something unpleasant."

"How could you know that?"

"Shall I say that your eyes are very revealing, or perhaps, more surprising, I can read your thoughts."

"But you must . . . not do . . . that."

"Why not?"

"Because it is an intrusion and I have no wish for anybody to know what I am thinking."

"Then tell me what I am thinking," the *Comte* suggested.

She looked up at him, saw the expression in his eyes and felt that if she put it into words it would sound very immodest and fast.

As if she had spoken the *Comte* said:

"Exactly! And there is no need for us to speak of what we both know."

Because she was so surprised by what he was saying Zena stumbled and missed a step.

"You are upsetting me!" she said accusingly.

"I have no wish to do that," the *Comte* replied. "Actually I am being very restrained, but needless to say every moment we are together I am growing more and more curious about you."

"That is ridiculous! This is supposed to be a light-hearted evening in which you just have to enjoy yourself."

"I am enjoying myself," the *Comte* insisted, "more than I thought possible and far more than I expected to do."

He smiled as he said:

"I arrived in Paris tonight feeling bored and thinking that although I had time to make contact with my friends I should be wise to go to bed early and start the social round of old acquaintances tomorrow."

His arms seemed to tighten for a moment around Zena's waist as he said:

"On an impulse I went to the Artists' Ball, and from that moment everything changed."

There was no need for her to ask what he

meant, but because she felt she must say something she remarked.

"I am glad you have found it amusing, and tomorrow you can start being social."

"Tomorrow I am going to see you," the *Comte* replied. "Can we have luncheon together?"

It flashed through Zena's mind that it would be very exciting to do so, but aloud she said:

"I must ask Kendric what our plans are. I really have no idea."

"Perhaps the *Vicomte*'s plans will not include you," the *Comte* suggested.

As he spoke Zena followed the direction of his eyes and saw with a little sense of shock that sitting at the end of the long table they had just left Kendric had his arms around Yvonne and was kissing her passionately.

It was in fact what the rest of the party had been doing all the evening, but Zena had felt it was a very strange way of behaving in a public place and had not expected it of her brother.

She looked away quickly and the *Comte* said:

"I am making plans to show you Paris because I am quite certain there is a lot we can see together that you would enjoy."

Zena did not reply and when they had been round the dance-floor once more the *Comte* took her back to the table and to her surprise left her while he went to speak to Kendric.

He talked to him for several minutes, then returned to say:

"The *Vicomte* has agreed that I should take

you home. I think you are tired, but he has no wish to leave."

"You are quite certain that Kendric does not wish me to stay until he is ready to go?" Zena asked.

The *Comte* smiled in a way she did not understand before he replied:

"Yes, in fact he was grateful to me for suggesting that I should look after you."

There was nothing Zena could do but agree, and while she was surprised that the *Comte* should be so solicitous, she was in fact growing a little tired because she had not slept much the night before.

She had been too excited and at the same time apprehensive in case Kendric's plans did not come off.

What was more, she had no wish to be so tired tomorrow that she would waste some of their precious free hours in sleeping.

The *Comte* put her wrap around her shoulders, and she was just about to walk to Kendric's side to say goodnight to him, when to her astonishment she saw that he too had risen from the table and was leaving through an exit at the end of the Dance-Hall which led into the Champs Élysées.

As she watched him and Yvonne climbing into one of the *fiacres* that were waiting for customers, she and the *Comte* followed them slowly and she saw the *fiacre* drive away.

"I wonder why Kendric is going on somewhere else," she said. "It was so pleasant here and much nicer than any other places we have been to."

She thought the *Comte* looked at her sharply, but he merely said:

"He asked me to say goodnight to you."

There was no need for Zena to reply because the *Comte* was hailing another *fiacre,* then helping her into it.

The roof was open and as they drove away Zena looked up at the stars to say:

"I always thought there would be a magic about Paris, and it is even more beautiful and more exciting than I imagined."

"I did ask you before if this was your first visit to Paris," the *Comte* said, and this time she answered quickly:

"My first since I was grown up."

"Which has not been very long," the *Comte* remarked.

Because she realised he was being inquisitive again she stopped looking up at the sky and said:

"You are trying to guess my age. I have always been told that is a rude and indiscreet thing to do."

"Only when women wish to conceal how old they are," the *Comte* replied, "and I know without your telling me that you are very young, both in years and experience."

"Now you *are* guessing," Zena said feeling she had to answer this assertion.

"I think, if the truth is known, I am reading your thoughts and using my instinct," the *Comte* said.

"I do not wish you to do either."

Although he had not moved she felt in some way that he was encroaching on her, becoming too intimate and, although she could not explain it, too possessive.

It was fortunately only a very short distance from where they had danced to where she and Kendric were staying, and as the horses stopped outside the tall mansion at the end of the Rue St. Honoré the *Comte* said:

"As these are private apartments, I imagine you and the *Vicomte* are staying with friends."

"We have been lent an apartment," Zena replied.

The *Comte* made no effort to open the carriage-door. Instead he turned sideways to say:

"Because I think you should go to bed quickly, I am not going to suggest that I escort you to the door of your apartment. Instead, because as you well know, we have a lot more to say to each other than we have been able to say tonight, I will call for you at half-after-noon tomorrow and we will have luncheon at a quiet Restaurant where we will not be disturbed."

Since this was something Zena was more than willing to do, she was just about to accept eagerly when she remembered Kendric.

"I must first ask . . ." she began.

"The *Vicomte* is of course included in my invitation, if he wishes to join us," the *Comte* said, "but I have a feeling that he may be entertaining somebody else."

In view of the way he had been behaving with Yvonne, Zena thought this was very likely, and as she had no wish to be left alone in the apartment with nowhere to go she said quickly:

"Then I should like to have luncheon with you. Thank you very much for asking me."

She put out her hand as she spoke and the *Comte* took it in both of his.

He did not speak, but he sat looking at her and she had a strange feeling that he was turning over in his mind whether he should say or do something or not.

Then as if he had come to a decision he raised her hand to his lips and kissed it as he had done before.

"Goodnight, Zena," he said. "I am glad I have been a part of your first night in Paris, and I intend to make sure that this is the first of many."

He kissed her hand again, his lips moving insistently on her skin.

Then he opened the carriage-door, helped her down on to the pavement and woke the Nightwatchman who was asleep in the Concierge's office.

Drowsily he handed Zena the key of the apartment, then went back to his chair, settled himself into it and closed his eyes.

Zena stood in the dark Hallway and the light

from the one gaslight made her hair shine as if it consisted of little tongues of fire.

The *Comte* looked at her for a long moment.

"Goodnight," he said and his voice was very deep.

"Goodnight and . . . thank you," Zena replied and turned away.

As she ran up the stairs without looking back she had the feeling that he was standing watching her go and wishing, as she did, that the evening had not come to an end.

Zena awoke and knew because the sun was shining golden into her room that it must be very late in the morning.

She could hardly believe it was true when she looked at the clock on the mantelpiece and saw it was nearly eleven o'clock. She could never remember sleeping so late before.

She remembered that when they arrived at the apartment the Concierge had said that when she wanted *petit déjeuner* she was to ring the bell, and either she or her daughter would bring it upstairs.

Zena was just about to ring the bell when she thought that perhaps Kendric had ordered his breakfast already and she opened the door into the Sitting-Room to go and ask him.

She wondered what time he had got back and was glad he had not awakened her.

She walked through the Sitting-Room and knocked on the door of his bedroom.

There was no response and she opened the door.

The first thing she saw was Kendrick's clothes thrown untidily over a chair, some of which had slid onto the floor.

Then she saw that he was in bed, fast asleep.

For a moment she hesitated as to whether she should waken him, then she thought it would be a mistake to do so.

Instead she went from the room, closed the door and rang for her own *petit déjeuner* wondering, if they should bring up breakfast for two, how she could keep Kendric's coffee hot until he awoke.

It was actually a long time before the Concierge's daughter Renée appeared carrying a tray.

There was steaming hot coffee in an open jug, croissants that were warm from the oven, butter, and jam made from *fraises des bois* to spread on them.

"*Bonjour, M'mselle,*" Renée said. "Did you have a nice time last night?"

"Wonderful, thank you," Zena replied.

"I heard you come in at four o'clock," Renée went on as she set the tray down on a table in the window, "but *Monsieur* was very, very late. He did not come back until seven o'clock this morning, and I guessed he would still be asleep."

"Seven o'clock!" Zena exclaimed. "I did not think even in Paris dancing went on so late."

She thought Renée looked at her in a rather

strange way. Then she said with a little laugh:

"I do not think *Monsieur* was dancing, *M'mselle!*"

She left the room and Zena puzzled over her words.

If Kendrick was not dancing then where could he have been, she wondered.

Then she told herself that he was obviously taking that attractive Frenchgirl home and she supposed they had stayed talking and perhaps drinking in her apartment until the morning.

Zena of course had not known the details of Kendric's escapade at home with the dancer, and she imagined her father and mother were so angry with him because he had left the Palace without anybody being aware of it.

Also a dancer would be considered by her mother to be very unsuitable company for a Crown Prince.

If Kendric had behaved with the dancer in the same manner as he had behaved with Yvonne last night, Zena could understand that her mother had been shocked.

'If Mama ever hears how Kendric is behaving in Paris,' she thought, 'she will be absolutely furious!'

Then she realised that also applied to her. She had danced with a man to whom she had not been formally introduced and what was more, she intended to have luncheon with him today alone, unless Kendric wished to accompany them.

The idea of her mother's anger was very intimidating. Then Zena told herself there was no reason why their behaviour should ever be discovered unless at this very moment the Baron and the Countess were bewailing their disappearance at the Palace.

"I am sure Kendric is right and they will not risk losing their positions by admitting their incompetence," she told herself consolingly.

At the same time, even to think about it was frightening.

She finished her breakfast, then went to her room to start dressing.

It was quite difficult without a maid to fasten her small corset which laced up at the back and she was certain that she would not be able to manage the buttons on her gown.

She therefore left it until the very last moment, thinking that Kendric must wake soon.

If she left him sleeping until twelve o'clock he would still only have had five hours, and if he had been awake all night she was sure he needed more.

She dressed her hair as best she could, thinking as she did so, that if they were to go out this evening she must ask the Concierge to engage a *Coiffeur* to call at the apartment.

She then chose one of her prettiest and most elaborate gowns to wear for luncheon with the *Comte* thinking as she did so that it was amusing to recall that it had been intended to be worn at the Royal Garden Party which took place every summer at the Palace.

Also the Arch-Duchess had said it would be suitable for the day of the *Prix d'Or* when the Duke of Faverstone's horse would be running.

'He would certainly be surprised if he was told I had worn it before in Paris when I was lunching alone with a French *Comte* whom I had met without any proper introduction at the Artists' Ball,' Zena thought.

It struck her that if the Duke became aware of her behaviour he might refuse to marry her.

That would be one way of getting rid of him. At the same time, if it was not the Duke, it might be some horrible German Prince like Georg and then her fate would be even worse.

"I am not going to worry," she told herself. "Just for these few days I will be simply Zena Bellefleur, and because I am of no social consequence whatsoever, I can behave as I wish."

She wondered whether as a *demi-mondaine*, which Kendric had said she was, she should behave as Yvonne had done, but she knew that as far as she was concerned it would be impossible.

How could she throw her arms round a man and kiss him and how could she dance in such an abandoned way?

How could she even flirt provocatively as she had noticed the women in the party doing last night with every man who talked to them?

She thought of the women she had seen at the *Café Anglais* who she suspected were of a far higher class than the girls at the Ball.

'I am sure they just sit and look beautiful,' she thought, 'while men pay them compliments and give them jewellery because they are like magnificent pictures which they can hang on the walls and enjoy.'

She had an idea that perhaps they did something else, but she did not know what it could be.

The clock on the mantelpiece had just struck twelve and she was thinking she would have to wake Kendric and ask if he wished to come out to luncheon with her and the *Comte* when she heard his door open and realised he was awake.

She had left her own door ajar so that she could hear him, and as he came into the Sitting-Room she gave a cry of delight and jumped to her feet.

"You are awake, Kendric! I am so glad! I thought you would sleep for ever!"

Kendric rubbed his eyes.

"That is what I would like to do," he yawned. "What time is it?"

"It is after twelve o'clock. Shall I ring for your breakfast, or will you wait until luncheontime?"

"I had better have some coffee," Kendric replied. "I drank so much last night that my head aches like hell!"

"Oh, Kendric, I am sorry!" Zena said. "I have some *Eau de Cologne* with me. I will put some on a handkerchief and perhaps that will make you feel better."

Kendric groaned and sat himself down in a chair by the window.

With his fair tousled hair he looked very young and almost as if he had just come from school.

Zena rang for his *petit déjeuner* and fetched a small bottle of *Eau de Cologne* and a handkerchief from her bedroom.

She put it against his forehead and he lay back in a chair with his eyes closed.

"Listen Kendric," Zena said, "the *Comte* has asked us out to luncheon and he will be here soon, but if you have no wish to come, he will take me alone."

Kendric opened his eyes.

"I have just remembered," he said, "I have promised to give Yvonne luncheon."

"Then you will not want me!"

Kendric gave her one of his mischievous smiles.

"To tell you the truth, I was wondering what I could do about you."

"Oh, that is all right," Zena said. "I will have luncheon with the *Comte* and I am glad he has asked me since I have no wish to interfere in your amusements."

"That is the right word for it!" Kendric said sitting up and looking much more like his usual self. "I do not mind telling you, Zena, I am rather smitten with her."

"I thought she was much more attractive than that other girl, Nanette."

"Of course she is, and certainly a cut above

that riff-raff we had in the box with us last night."

Zena had thought the same thing and she said a little tentatively because she did not wish to seem as if she was prying:

"Is Yvonne an . . . actress?"

There was a pause before Kendric answered:

"I believe she has been on the stage at one time or another."

"And what is she doing now?"

Again there was a pause before her brother replied:

"I really have not had time to ask her a lot of questions."

"No . . . of course not," Zena said, "and it was very difficult to talk to anybody last night. The bands were so noisy, especially at that place in Montmartre."

"It was not the sort of place I should have gone to when you were with me," Kendric said, "but I had no idea it would be like that until we got there."

"I thought the last place in the Champs Élysées was lovely!" Zena said, "but I was surprised you did not say goodnight to me."

Her brother looked shame-facedly.

"To tell you the truth, Zena," he said, "I forgot."

He took the handkerchief from his forehead and added:

"The trouble is, I ought not to have brought you with me, but it is too late now."

"Of course it is!" Zena agreed. "Do not worry about me, I am enjoying every moment, and the *Comte* was very kind."

She thought Kendric looked at her suspiciously.

"He behaved properly towards you?" he asked sharply. "He did not try to kiss you, or — anything like that?"

"No, of course not!" Zena said. "He kissed my hand, but there is nothing wrong in that."

"No," Kendric agreed a little doubtfully, "but keep him at arms' length. You know what these Frenchmen are like."

Zena smiled.

"Actually, I have no idea what Frenchmen are like, but it is rather exciting to find out!"

Kendric groaned.

"Now, Zena, I warn you! If you do anything outrageous, I swear I shall take you straight to Ettengen!"

"Oh, Kendric! No! As though I would let you do that! I promise you I will never do anything of which you would disapprove, and you are very lucky I do not extract the same promise from you."

"*Touché!*" Kendric laughed, "but I am thinking of that ghastly Barracks and storing up a few memories with which I can cheer myself up."

"I am doing exactly the same thing!" Zena said.

They smiled at each other as if there was no

need to put it into words that twins always thought alike.

Then Kendric's *petit déjeuner* appeared.

As Renée set it down in front of him, Zena asked:

"Please, while you are here, would you be kind enough to do up my gown?"

"Of course, *M'mselle*. Which one are you going to wear?"

She went towards the bedroom and when Zena would have followed her Kendric gave a low whistle which made her stop.

"You must tip her," he whispered.

Zena looked surprised, then she realised it was something she should have done before.

"Yes, of course," she said. "How much?"

Kendric shrugged his shoulders.

"Two or three francs."

Zena nodded and went into the bedroom.

When Renée had helped her into her gown and buttoned it down the back she fumbled in her handbag and produced three francs.

"Thank you very much for helping me," she said.

She felt a little shy as she gave the girl the tip, having never in her life tipped anybody because whenever they travelled or went anywhere there was always the Countess or another lady-in-waiting to do it for her.

Renée seemed almost to snatch the tip, saying as she did so:

*"Merci beaucoup, M'mselle!"*

When she had left her Zena put her head round the door of the Sitting-Room to say to her brother:

"You must remember to tell me the things I have to do as a . . . commoner. That was the first time I had ever tipped anyone."

"Well, remember you must tip for any service, however small," Kendric said, "and if you do forget, the French will not be slow in reminding you."

The way he spoke made Zena ask:

"What did last night cost you?"

"I had to pay my share everywhere we went," Kendric replied, "and it came to more money than I expected. It is doubtful if you will be able to visit Worth."

"I would rather visit the Restaurants and Dance-Halls," Zena replied, "and don't forget I have a little money with me, and of course my jewellery."

"If you sold any of that you would be mad!" Kendric exclaimed. "If anything was missing it would be noticed as soon as you returned, and there would be an inquisition! You would soon find yourself confessing everything we have done."

Zena gave a cry of horror and disappeared back into her bedroom.

She put on the bonnet which went with her gown and thought as she looked at herself in the mirror that with her red lips and her darkened eyelashes it would be difficult for anybody in

Wiedenstein to recognise her.

"Nobody will ever know," she told her reflection consolingly.

As she did so she heard the door of the Sitting-Room open and Renée's voice say:

"A gentleman to see you, *Monsieur!*"

Zena's heart gave a leap because she knew who it would be before she heard the *Comte*'s deep voice say:

"Good-morning, Villerny, I see you slept late."

"Yes, very late," Kendric replied, "and thank you for taking my . . ."

He hesitated and Zena held her breath.

She knew that without thinking, and perhaps because he was sleepy, Kendric had been about to say 'my sister'.

Then he substituted 'Zena' and as he said the rest of the sentence she moved into the Sitting-Room.

The *Comte*, looking even more impressive than he had last night, was standing at the window beside Kendric.

Because the sunshine was behind him she felt that he was enveloped in light.

"*Bonjour Monsieur!*" she said demurely.

The *Comte* turned to face her, and she thought from the expression in his eyes that he appreciated her gown, her bonnet and her skilfully painted face.

"Good-morning, Zena," he said. "There is no need for me to ask you if you slept well! You look like Spring itself!"

"That is how I feel," Zena replied, "but poor Kendric has a headache, and therefore has no wish to accompany us."

"I am sorry about your head, but it is not surprising. If you drank the champagne at that low Dance-Hall in Montmartre," the *Comte* said, "it is only a miracle you are alive!"

"I was foolish enough to drink at least two glasses," Kendric said, "but I was thirsty."

The *Comte* smiled in what Zena thought was a slightly superior manner, and she said quickly:

"Kendric was saying just now that we should not have gone to such a place."

"*You* certainly should not have done so," the *Comte* answered, accentuating the first word.

"You are preaching at me in a somewhat obscure fashion," Kendric interposed. "I must leave you or I shall be late for my own luncheon date."

He rose and as he walked towards his bedroom Zena said:

"What time will you be back here? When shall I see you again?"

"I will be back before dinner," Kendric said carelessly. "I have not yet decided where we shall dine. I have had various invitations, but I have not yet answered any of them."

"I was hoping," the *Comte* said, "that you and Zena would dine with me."

Kendric reached his bedroom door and turned round.

"May I leave the invitation open until later today?" he asked.

He did not wait for an answer but smiled at his sister and went into his bedroom. Only as Zena turned back to the *Comte* did she see that he was looking surprised.

Because she felt he might ask her questions she did not want to answer, she said:

"Shall we go? It seems a pity to be indoors when the sun is shining."

She picked up the handbag which matched her gown and started to put on her long kid gloves as she walked ahead of the *Comte* towards the door.

He hurried to open it for her and as he did so, he said:

"Shall I tell you how lovely you are looking, or shall I wait until we are at the place I have chosen for us to have luncheon?"

"I am quite prepared to wait," Zena replied, "but I find compliments embarrassing and I would much rather you did not make them."

As they went out of the apartment closing the door behind them he asked:

"If what you have said about compliments is true, then you are very different from any other woman in the whole of Paris!"

"I have always heard that compliments from Frenchmen are too glib to be sincere," Zena said, "and I am beginning to think that is true."

The *Comte* did not answer, and as she went through the door into the street, she saw in surprise that there was not an ordinary *voiture* waiting for them, but a very elegant private carriage with a coachman on the box and a footman to open the door.

Zena stepped into it and sat down on the soft cushioned seats.

"This is very grand!" she exclaimed.

"It is a very much more suitable conveyance for you than those in which we travelled last night," the *Comte* replied.

She wanted to ask him if he owned it or had hired it, then thought that would seem impertinent, but as if again he was reading her thoughts the *Comte* said:

"I have borrowed it from one of my friends, and I am glad you appreciate it."

Because she thought that he was insinuating that because she was of no social importance she usually travelled behind inferior horses, Zena longed to tell him she was used to Royal Carriages, and that her father's stable was famous in Wiedenstein.

Then she told herself that if the *Comte* had the slightest suspicion of who she was the whole excitement of being alone with this man who treated her as an ordinary woman would be changed.

After the formality of the Court and the way the Countess, the Statesmen and the Courtiers spoke to her, it was fascinating to find the *Comte* addressing her as she supposed Kendric addressed Yvonne and the other women with whom he associated.

94

Because she too was for the moment free of Royal restrictions, she smiled at the *Comte* and said with a little lilt in her voice:

"It is very exciting to be in Paris and to be with you. Please tell me where we are going."

"To a small Restaurant in the Bois which has only just opened," the *Comte* replied, "and has not yet become fashionable. The big ones where we would see all the world and his wife are not for us, not today at any rate."

She looked at him enquiringly, and he said:

"I would like to go to them to show you off, but I might meet friends who would want to talk to me and to you, and today I want a *tête-à-tête* where there are no interruptions, except for the song of the birds."

"It sounds very romantic!" Zena said without thinking.

"That is exactly what I intend it to be!" the *Comte* agreed in his deep voice.

# Chapter Four

Afterwards Zena was to think that her luncheon in the Bois with the *Comte* were the most enchanting hours she had ever known.

The Restaurant to which he took her was small with a little one-storey house which was surrounded by a garden filled with shady trees.

There were only about a dozen tables among the flowers, and the Proprietor, who was also the Chef, took the orders himself and spent a long time explaining which speciality would be the best for his clients on that particular day.

His wife, buxom in black, made out the bills, and their two sons were the waiters.

There was a happy atmosphere about the whole place and to Zena it was something she had never experienced before and felt despairingly she would never do again.

When the *Comte* had ordered and the wine was brought in a bucket filled with ice he turned to smile at her and said:

"Now all we have to do is to enjoy eating what I am sure will be an extremely good luncheon, and being — together."

96

The way he spoke made Zena feel excited and she answered:

"I am enjoying every moment of my visit to Paris, and you know I want to thank you for looking after me last night."

"I am determined that you will not go to such places again or meet the dregs of Paris," the *Comte* replied, and there was a hard note in his voice.

Zena did not reply and he went on:

"I intend to speak to the *Vicomte* about it and I hope you will not try to prevent me."

Zena gave a little cry.

"Please do not speak to Kendric!" she said. "He was, I think, a little ashamed of himself this morning, besides feeling ill from the bad wine he drank, and as I was with you I did not mind seeing how those other women behaved."

"All the same," the *Comte* said, "you are too good for this sort of thing."

"I am glad you think so."

"What I cannot understand," he went on, "is why de Villerny brought you to Paris in the first place if he did not intend to spend his time with you."

Zena looked away across the garden.

She was afraid this was one of the things the *Comte* would ask.

She knew that it must seem strange, if she was Kendric's *Chère Amie,* that he should be prepared to leave her at the Dance-Hall without even saying goodnight.

Now, because she thought that anything she might reply would make matters sound even stranger than they were already, she said quickly:

"Please . . . can we talk about more . . . interesting things? It is so exciting to be here with you, and it is something I will want to remember when I have gone home."

The *Comte* stiffened.

"You are thinking of leaving?"

"We shall have to go in a day or two."

"You mean the *Vicomte* will have to leave. But surely you are not compelled to go with him?"

"If he leaves, I must leave," Zena said firmly, "but I do not want to talk about it. I want you to tell me about yourself. Do you realise I have no idea where you live or even where you are staying in Paris?"

The *Comte* smiled.

"I am glad it is of interest to you. I am staying in Paris in a very beautiful house on the Champs Élysées belonging to the *Duc* de Soissons. I wish I could show you his pictures. He has the most famous collection in France."

"I would love to see them," Zena said, "and while I am here I must visit the Louvre. I always think Fragonard and Boucher painted the most romantic pictures anyone could imagine."

"You have obviously seen some of their work already," the *Comte* said.

Zena looked at him almost defiantly.

"We are not entirely uncivilized in Wiedenstein."

He laughed softly.

"So you are a patriot! I like people to be patriotic and proud of their own country."

"I am very proud of mine," Zena said, "even though it is small and not a great nation compared to France or Prussia."

"And yet it is at this moment of considerable importance in Europe," the *Comte* said. "Do you know why?"

"Of course I do," Zena replied. "If Prussia invades France, which many people are afraid may happen, then Wiedenstein, like Switzerland, must be neutral, which may be difficult."

She spoke positively because she had heard her father and the other Statesmen in Wiedenstein discuss this subject so often. Then as the *Comte* did not speak she went on:

"I cannot bear to think of the Prussians marching into France. Suppose they tried to destroy this beautiful city?"

"I feel exactly the same way," the *Comte* said, "and I wish you could speak to the Emperor as you are speaking to me."

"Papa says he is under the thumb of the Empress who is great friends with the Foreign Minister who hates Bismarck so bitterly that he is longing to fight him."

She spoke without thinking, then she gave a sudden exclamation:

"I have just realised that the Foreign Minister is the *Duc* de Graumont, and that is your name!"

"That is true," the *Comte* replied. "But the de Graumonts are a very large family and I am only a very distant cousin of the *Duc*."

There was a pause. Then Zena said:

"Perhaps I have been . . . indiscreet. I apologise . . . please forget what I have . . . said."

Even as she spoke she realised that an apology was quite unnecessary.

It would have been very reprehensible for the Princess Marie-Thérèse to have made such remarks, but anything Zena Bellefleur said or thought was not of the least consequence.

"I hope we may always be frank with each other," the *Comte* answered, "and I was just thinking that it is quite unnecessary for you to be clever as well as beautiful."

Zena gave a little laugh.

"What you are really saying is that you like women who are pretty dolls . . . playthings which are easily discarded when you have no further use for them."

She was thinking of how Kendric thought that the only important thing about a woman was that she should be pretty.

Once when Zena had asked him what he talked about with his dancer had replied scornfully:

"Talk? Why should I want to talk to somebody like that? All that mattered was that she was pretty, and I wanted to kiss her."

Now as if the *Comte* realised she was thinking of Kendric he said:

"What do you talk about when he is not making love to you?"

Zena felt herself stiffen, and instinctively she felt insulted that he should say anything so personal to her or suspect that she allowed any man to talk of love as he had done last night.

Then once again she remembered who she was supposed to be.

"We were not talking about Kendric," she said aloud after what seemed a long silence, "but about you."

"But I would much rather talk about you," the *Comte* replied, "and before you interrupt me I am going to say again that I have never met anybody so lovely, or so enchanting."

Enchanting was the right word for everything they said and everything they did, Zena thought as they drove home.

They had sat over luncheon until everybody else had left the Restaurant, then sitting in the comfortable open carriage which Zena now guessed belonged to the *Duc* de Soissons they drove along the side of the Seine as far as Notre Dame.

Then they returned through the small narrow streets of old Paris until they reached the impressive boulevards which had been built by Baron Haussmann.

It was so beautiful and so exciting that it seemed quite natural that the *Comte* should hold her hand while Zena looked around her.

She thought perhaps she should prevent him from doing so, but to do so seemed rather childish and so they drove side by side and hand-in-hand until the horses drew up outside her apartment.

"May I come in?" the *Comte* asked. "And if de Villerny is back, I can ask if he has made up his mind whether you will dine with me this evening."

"Please do that," Zena replied, "and I do hope Kendric says yes."

"You cannot possibly want it as much as I do," the *Comte* smiled.

The Concierge gave them the key of the apartment which meant that Kendric was not yet back, and they went up the stairs to the first floor.

The *Comte* opened the door for Zena and they went into the attractive Sitting-Room where the sun was shining through the windows.

"Kendric is not yet back," Zena explained unnecessarily, "but I hope you will wait here with me."

"I have every intention of doing so," the *Comte* replied.

Zena put down her gloves and handbag on a chair, then pulled off her fashionable bonnet.

Then as she turned she found that the *Comte* was standing just beside her and as once again he had his back to the sunlight he looked, as he had this morning, as if he was enveloped with light.

They stood looking at each other, and Zena had no idea how it happened, whether she moved or he did, but some strange power that was outside themselves and their minds drew them together.

The *Comte*'s arms went round her, and as she looked up at him wonderingly his lips came down on hers.

She had never been kissed, but she had often thought that if she loved somebody it would be very wonderful, and the feeling of the *Comte*'s lips was indeed wonderful, but so much more.

They were magical, enchanted, and his kiss seemed an extension of the strange sensations he aroused in her ever since they had first met.

And yet, in a way she could not explain to herself, although her feelings had been strange, they had yet been part of her dreams, and what she had always sought.

Now as his arms tightened around her and his lips became more insistent, she knew this was what she had always wanted in life and it was although she was afraid to admit it . . . love.

It was love that had nothing to do with position or advantage, but was instead the meeting of a man and woman who belonged to each other and while their hearts and their spirits merged there was no need for words.

The *Comte* drew her closer still and now Zena felt as if her whole body vibrated to his and a rapture that was inexpressible seemed to run through her like the warmth of the sun and sweep up through her breasts to move from her lips to his.

The room swung round them and she felt as if her feet were no longer on the ground, but that the *Comte* was carrying her on the shaft of sunlight into the glory and wonder of Heaven.

Only when Zena felt as if she was no longer herself but his, and it was impossible to think but only to feel, did the *Comte* raise his head.

For a moment he looked down at her eyes shining with a radiance that seemed almost blinding, her cheeks flushed against the whiteness of her skin, and her lips parted from the insistence of his.

There was no need to speak; the *Comte* knew that Zena's heart was beating tumultuously against him.

He knew too that this kiss was very different from any kiss he had ever known before.

Then he was kissing her again; kissing her with long, slow, passionate kisses which left them both trembling at the same time ecstatic and once again journeying towards the heart of the sun.

A long time later, as if the *Comte* felt they could no longer stand locked in each other's arms but needed support, he drew Zena to the sofa.

As they sat down she raised her eyes to his and he said:

"Could anybody be more perfect, more

alluring? But, my precious, I must talk to you."

Even as he spoke they heard footsteps outside the door and as it opened and Kendric came in, the *Comte* moved a little way from Zena.

"I am sorry to be late," Kendric exclaimed, throwing his top-hat down on a chair, "but I have been seeing a number of Philippe's friends, and I have a marvellous invitation for us this evening."

"Invita . . . tion?" Zena asked in a voice that did not sound like her own.

The *Comte* rose slowly to his feet.

"That sounds as if you do not intend to accept mine," he said.

"I am sorry, de Graumont," Kendric replied, "perhaps we can dine with you tomorrow night, but we have been asked, Zena and I, to have dinner with Prince Napoleon, which as you are aware, is a Royal Command, and to go on later to a party to be given by *La Païva* at her house in the Champs Élysées, and that too is something we cannot miss!"

The *Comte* frowned.

"I did not think you knew the Prince Napoleon."

Kendric laughed.

"I met him today for the first time with one of Philippe's friends. He told me he was giving a dinner-party tonight at his house and he had been informed I had a very beautiful lady-friend whom he was anxious to meet."

Kendric looked at Zena as he spoke and added:

"I could hardly say to the Prince that you would prefer to dine with somebody else."

"N . . . no . . . of course not," Zena agreed.

"At the same time," the *Comte* said, "you know the Prince's reputation with women? I do not feel he is the right sort of man for Zena."

Kendric shrugged his shoulders.

"I will look after Zena," he said, "and it would be impossible, as I have accepted His Royal Highness's invitation, to back out now."

Zena was aware that the *Comte* was apprehensive and it was with difficulty that he did not make any further protest about Kendric's arrangements.

Because she felt it might be uncomfortable if he did so, she held out her hand.

"I am so sorry we cannot dine with you to-night," she said, "but please, I would like to accept for tomorrow evening, if you will have us."

"I will see you before that," the *Comte* answered. "You have already promised that you will let me take you to the Louvre tomorrow morning."

Zena's eyes lit up.

"Yes, of course," she said, "and I know Kendric does not like Museums or Picture Galleries, so we can start early."

"I will call for you at eleven o'clock," the *Comte* promised, "and thank you for a very happy day."

He raised her hand to his lips and she thought as he kissed it he said without words how much he minded leaving her and how very wonderful their day had been.

Then there was nothing the *Comte* could do now but leave, and when he had gone Kendric exclaimed:

"Zena! I have so much to tell you! Tonight will be extremely interesting even though your friend de Graumont disapproves."

He did not wait for Zena to make any remark, but went on to explain that the Prince Napoleon's parties, which he had always longed to attend, were the most sought after in Paris.

"He can only give them at his home while his wife is away in the country," Kendric explained, "and then he invites all the most famous women in the city."

"Women like those we saw at the *Café Anglais?*" Zena asked.

"Exactly!" Kendric agreed. "And although I suppose it is wrong for you to do so, you will see the most celebrated of the Courtesans who have made Paris the El Dorado of every man in Europe, although their wives and mothers call it something very different!"

"And that, I am sure, includes Mama!"

Kendric flung up his hands.

"She would kill me if she ever finds out where I have taken you!" he said. "But what you will see tonight and the women you will meet will certainly be an education in itself, although it is something you have to forget the moment you go home."

When she was dressing for dinner, Zena admitted to herself that she not only much preferred to be with the *Comte* but also that she loved him.

The word frightened her, and yet she knew he had stolen her heart, and it would never again belong to her or to any other man.

"I love him!" she whispered, and knew that her love was hopeless and could end in nothing but heart-break.

Yet it was an ecstasy to know that he could arouse her to such an inexpressible rapture and that tomorrow she would see him again.

Tomorrow and for five more days!

Then for the rest of her life she would have nothing but memories and the misery of knowing that although they were both in the same world they were divided by a chasm as deep as the English Channel and there was nothing they could do to bridge it.

'Perhaps one day, when I am miserable and lonely in England,' she thought, 'I may see him again. But if I did what would it do except make me more unhappy than I was already?'

Then she told herself that somehow after tonight she would contrive to be with the *Comte* every moment they were in Paris and she would tell Kendric to accept no more invitations on her behalf.

When she was dressed in one of the gowns that the Arch-Duchess had bought for her to wear at the Ball which would be given in race-week, she thought when she had mascaraed her eyelashes and reddened her lips that she would not look too insignificant among the Prince Napoleon's other lady guests.

She had no wish to arouse his admiration, or that of any other man present, but she did not wish to let Kendric down or make those who had arranged to have them both invited to the Prince's party think that his interests in women were inferior to theirs.

She knew as she went into the Sitting-Room that Kendric was nervous in case she would look too ladylike.

His eyes went first to her head.

The *Coiffeur* had fortunately arrived when Zena was nearly dressed and had made her red-gold hair even more sensational than it usually was.

He had also arranged in it three diamond brooches in the shape of stars and they glittered with every movement she made.

She had clasped around her neck a diamond necklace which her mother had told her not to wear until she was married, as it was too large for a young girl.

Kendric's eyes lingered on the necklace and he said with a smile:

"When you are asked, do not forget to say that I gave you that! It will certainly enhance my prestige, although if anybody knew me well they would wonder how I could afford it!"

Zena was just about to ask him if he had given

Yvonne a present. Then she thought he might think she was questioning his generosity and decided that in any case there would be no necessity for it as he had known her for only a short time.

Therefore she said nothing and Kendric afraid of being late hurried her downstairs.

To her surprise she found that her brother had hired a carriage to take them to the Prince Napoleon's house.

"You are being very grand!" she said.

"It is expensive but worth it," Kendric replied, "I dislike seeming like a poor relation and I do not mind telling you that some of Philippe's friends, because I am from Wiedenstein, are rather patronizing."

Zena laughed.

"They would not be that if they knew who you were!"

Kendric laughed too.

"I almost feel like telling them."

"Do be careful!" she begged.

"Do not worry, drunk or sober, that is one secret I shall not reveal!" Kendric said. "And you be careful too what you say to de Graumont. I have a feeling he is growing rather fond of you."

"Why should you think that?" Zena asked.

"I thought he was jealous because I was taking you to dine with the Prince, and the way he looked at you might have been admiration, or it might have been something else."

"He has been very kind," Zena said quickly,

"and we had a very interesting talk at luncheon."

As she spoke she realised it was the first time in her life she had had any secrets from her twin brother.

She did not want Kendric to know that the *Comte* had kissed her, or in fact that she loved him.

Never had Zena thought that women could be so beautiful, so superbly gowned, or wear so many expensive jewels.

But, and it was a very large 'but', she was absolutely astounded how common was their manner of speaking.

The men were all distinguished with high-sounding titles, and Zena did not have to hear them speak to know that they represented the cream of the French aristocracy as well as holding important posts in the Government.

But the women were not all of French origin, there were also two English women and a Russian.

Zena could not tell from the way the Russian spoke if she was cultured or not, but the French-women did not only speak without Parisian accents, but in their conversation used an argot that was incomprehensible to her, while the two English women spoke in a manner that would have made her mother refuse to engage them as kitchen-maids.

For the first time Zena thought she understood why Kendric had said that while he was with the dancer he did not talk to her.

What could these distinguished and obviously very intelligent men have in common with such women who mispronounced the most ordinary words and who had only to open their red lips to sound vulgar?

She was so bemused while at the same time curious about them, that she sat at the dinner-table looking round, forgetting for the moment to be polite and talk to the gentleman on her right.

Kendric was on her left and she realised they were seated together because the men and women who had been announced after their own arrival were also paired round the dinner-table.

The Prince's partner was obviously prepared to act as hostess, and she looked so sensational and was so loaded down with jewels that Zena thought she was like a Prima Donna on a stage, determined to take all the applause for herself.

"Will you tell me your name, pretty lady?" Zena heard.

She turned to see there was a middle-aged man beside her who had an interesting but, she thought, rather debauched face.

There were lines of dissipation under his eyes that were dark and penetrating and although he had a clever forehead below slightly greying hair, that too was lined with age.

"My name is Zena, *Monsieur*."

"Why have I not met you before?" the gentleman asked.

"I have only just come to Paris."

"Then that accounts for it. I may tell you that my parties, and I am the Marquis de Sade, are as famous as our host's, and I hope you will do me the honour of being my guest."

"That is very kind of you, *Monsieur*."

As Zena spoke she was quite certain she had heard of the *Marquis* de Sade but in what particular connection she could not be sure.

He bent nearer to her and as she met his eyes she decided she did not like him.

She could not explain why, but the feeling was there that he was a man she should not trust.

"Am I to understand that you are under the protection of de Villerny?" the *Marquis* enquired.

Zena avoided replying to his question by sipping her wine from the twisted glass engraved with the Prince Napoleon's insignia.

"He is too young for you," the *Marquis* went on. "With your hair I know that, when a man can ignite them, the fires of love can burn fiercely and all-consumingly, but it is unlikely that de Villerny is the right man to do so."

"What I would like you to do," Zena said, "is to tell me the names of these outstanding people around the table. Being a stranger I should love to know who they are."

She thought she was very clever in sidetracking the *Marquis* into a different subject, but he merely smiled and replied:

"I want to talk of you, and of course, myself. Tell me how long you have known de Villerny?"

113

"For a very long time," Zena said defiantly, "and we are very happy together."

Both those things were true, she thought, and as she spoke she could hear her voice ring with sincerity.

"I have a very charming house near the Bois which is empty at the moment," the *Marquis* said. "I want to show it to you."

Zena did not reply and he went on:

"Tomorrow we will go together to Oscar Massin's, and you shall choose for yourself one of his flower-jewelled brooches which are without exception the finest in the world."

Because the way he spoke made Zena feel not only uncomfortable but a little afraid, she said:

"I do not . . . understand what you are saying to me, *Monsieur le Marquis* and if I try to do so . . . I think . . . perhaps it will make me . . . angry."

The *Marquis* laughed.

"You are very young, but you are intelligent enough to know that I am suggesting you change your present protector for one who will make you one of the most famous women in France, in fact a Queen of your own profession."

Zena felt she could not have heard him aright.

Then she thought that just as Kendric had explained to her that the women of Paris received jewels and gowns from men so that they could parade them like racehorses to arouse the envy of their friends, so the women were prepared to accept such gifts from the highest bidder.

114

'I must not be angry,' she told herself, 'I must merely refuse the *Marquis*'s offer politely, but firmly.'

That was however easier said than done, for she realised that the *Marquis* had apparently made up his mind the moment he saw her that he wanted her, and that he was a man who always got what he wanted in one way or another, and who had no intention of accepting a refusal where she was concerned.

Whatever protests she made to him he did not listen, and when finally they left the Dining-Room she found not only his behaviour incomprehensible but also that of the other guests at the Prince's table.

As the meal progressed she realised that all the men present were behaving in a more and more familiar manner with the women next to them, and the only odd man out appeared to be Kendric who had become absorbed with the lady on his left.

This was possible because the Prince Napoleon had two women to amuse him, not only the one who was prepared to act as hostess, but also a very celebrated actress whose witty remarks managed to keep her host laughing and also to hold enthralled the gentleman on her other side.

This left his partner free for Kendric and he was certainly making the most of it.

In the French fashion, both men and women left the Dining-Room together and Zena took the opportunity of keeping close to the other ladies as they went up the stairs to collect their wraps, for they were all going on to the party given by La Païva.

When she came downstairs again, to Zena's relief she saw Kendric standing alone and reached him before any other woman could do so.

"Do not leave me alone with the *Marquis* de Sade," she begged. "He is being rather tiresome."

"I have heard about him," Kendric said. "Have nothing to do with him! If he gets difficult I shall take you home."

Zena was just about to say that perhaps that would be a good idea anyway when all the other women appeared.

Before it was possible to say anything more to her brother she found they were squeezed into a carriage with two other people and could not have a conversation without being overheard.

Fortunately the other couple were immersed in each other, and as the man kissed and fondled the woman in a way that Zena found most embarrassing, at least, she thought, she was free of the *Marquis*'s attentions.

When she had refused to hold his hand at dinner she had felt his knee pressing against hers, and had to twist herself to avoid such advances.

It was not a very long distance to La Païva's house and Kendric told her that it was the most luxurious private mansion in Paris and had taken ten years to build.

When they entered it there were loud voices and the fragrance of expensive perfume seemed to make it different from any house Zena had ever been in before.

There was a vast Salon lit by five tall windows, with a magnificent ceiling depicting 'Night' chasing 'Day' away. The walls were hung with crimson brocade and it seemed almost like a Temple dedicated to pleasure.

Before this Zena had followed the other ladies up the stairs which were lit by a massive lustre in sculptured bronze, and she saw to her astonishment that the steps and bannister were made entirely of onyx.

They left their coats in a bedroom where the bed was inlaid with rare woods and ivory, and stood like an altar in an alcove.

"That cost 100,000 francs!" she heard one of the guests say, and the voice was sharp with envy.

There were many other things that Zena would have liked to look at, but she was afraid that if she was away from Kendric for too long she would find that the lady who had been his neighbour at dinner might once again monopolise him.

She therefore hurried down the onyx staircase and when she reached the Salon she saw to her consternation that the *Marquis* de Sade and Kendric were speaking angrily to each other.

She hurried to her brother's side and as she did so he said:

"I have told you, *Monsieur le Marquis*, that Zena is mine, and I have no intention of giving her up to you, or to anybody else!"

Zena's heart missed a beat, and because the *Marquis* looked not only extremely angry but also overpowering, she slipped her hand into Kendric's.

"I have already told him, Kendric," she said in a low voice, "that we belong to each other, and that I will never leave you."

"Then surely that is decisive enough for you?" Kendric said to the *Marquis*.

He spoke in rather a loud voice and Zena realised that he had had a lot to drink and was annoyed and affronted by the *Marquis*'s behaviour.

There was a Band playing, and Zena said, pulling at her brother's hand:

"Let us go and dance, Kendric."

"Not so fast!" the *Marquis* de Sade said. "I have already made an offer of jewellery to this pretty songbird and I presume you are expecting me to ante-up on the original sum I had suggested! Very well then, I will double it!"

"I consider that an insult!" Kendric said.

The *Marquis* smiled, and it was a very unpleasant sight.

"If I have insulted you, it will be quite easy for you to obtain an apology in the time-honoured manner."

As he spoke Zena knew exactly what he was suggesting, and gave a cry of horror.

Even as she did so, she was aware that some-body had come to her side, and without even turning her head she knew who it was and felt a sense of relief that was also an indescribable joy.

Without pausing to think she turned to move close to the *Comte* and say in a whisper she thought only he would hear:

"Stop him! Please . . . stop him! Kendric must not fight a duel with him! Please . . . please . . . prevent it!"

There was a note of agony in her voice as she realised in terror what it would mean if Kendric fought a duel and was wounded, and it was dis-covered who he really was.

Because she was quick-witted, even as the *Marquis* had spoken and she had seen the smile on his lips, she knew he had been thinking that if he disabled Kendric it would be easier for him to take her from him.

As if he understood what she was feeling the *Comte* moved closer to the *Marquis* and said:

"I must request you, de Sade, to stop making yourself objectionable to these young people who are friends of mine."

"How dare you interrupt?" the *Marquis* said, diverted for the moment from his anger with Kendric. "What has it got to do with you?"

"It has a great deal to do with me," the *Comte* replied, "because I intend to protect *Mademoi-selle* Zena from men like you who are treating her as if she was a piece of merchandise to be hag-gled over in a degrading manner which any decent man would resent!"

The way he spoke was even more forceful than what he said and the *Marquis* seemed to go almost black with rage as he snarled:

"How dare you insult me and poke your nose into things which do not concern you!"

"I have already said they do concern me," the *Comte* replied, "and if you are intent on fighting anybody, then it would be more sportsmanlike to choose somebody of your own size, and fight me!"

"I will fight you both, if that is what you want," the *Marquis* shouted, "and when I have done so this young woman will be mine without any more argument about it."

"That is something she will never be!" Kendric said furiously.

Zena realised that it was a mistake for him to say anything, and as her fingers tightened on the *Comte*'s she knew he understood.

"I think the best thing I could do would be to take Zena home," he said to Kendric. "There is no reason why she should stay here and listen to a man who cannot behave like a gentleman."

"Thank you," Kendric said.

The *Marquis* gave a roar of rage.

"Do not dare to be so high-handed with me!" he said. "*Mademoiselle* Zena has already promised that she will accept my protection and I will therefore take her home."

He held out his arm as he spoke and Zena shrank back against the *Comte*.

"Come," the *Comte* said, and turned towards the door drawing her with him.

The *Marquis* however prevented her.

He seized Zena by the wrist and put his arm around her waist.

"You know on which side your bread is buttered, my pretty one!" he said. "Now tell these *imbeciles* once and for all that you have made your choice."

"No . . . No!" Zena cried and tried to release herself from the *Marquis*.

Now she was thoroughly frightened not only for herself, but for Kendric who had moved forward angrily to push the *Marquis* away from her.

"How dare you touch Zena!" he said. "Surely you realise she does not want you? If you do not leave her alone I will kick you out into the street!"

The *Marquis* turned round furiously and raised his arm as if he would hit Kendric.

Then as it flashed through Zena's mind that a duel between them was inevitable, the *Comte* acted.

"Kindly learn to behave yourself, *Monsieur le Marquis!*" he said, and slapped him across the face.

Now the *Marquis* seemed to go pale with anger.

"I will meet you at dawn," he said, "in the usual place, and when I have disposed of you I am perfectly prepared to take on this young jackanapes!"

"I accept your challenge!" the *Comte* said, "and what happens afterwards remains to be seen!"

The *Marquis* drew himself up with a look which told Zena he was very sure of victory.

"At five o'clock then," he said and walked away.

Zena gave a little murmur of horror, but it was impossible to speak because the *Comte* was moving her down the steps from the Salon into the Hall.

When he reached it he said to a servant:

"Fetch this lady's wrap."

The man bowed and waited for Zena to explain what it looked like.

Then as he hurried up the stairs she turned to the *Comte,* holding on to his arm with both hands.

"It is all right," he said softly. "Say nothing until we are away from here."

Zena therefore remained silent until the servant returned with her cloak and she stepped into the *Comte*'s carriage that was waiting outside.

As they drove away she threw herself against him, and his arms went around her as she hid her face against his shoulder.

"What can I say . . . how can I thank . . . you?" she asked. "It would be . . . impossible for Kendric to fight a duel . . . and anyway, I am certain that the *Marquis* would have been too . . . good for . . . him."

"The *Marquis* is considered one of the best shots in the country," the *Comte* said.

"Oh . . . no!" Zena cried, "in which case you must not fight him either!"

"That is something I must do," the *Comte* said.

"B . . . but . . . he may . . . injure you."

"That is a risk I have to take, but let me tell you that I am not afraid."

"No, of course not," Zena said, "but I should not have . . . involved you in this. It was only that I was so desperately . . . worried for . . . Kendric."

She thought as she spoke that if only she could explain that Kendric was the Crown Prince of Wiedenstein it would be easier.

"He is far too young to be involved with a man like de Sade," the *Comte* said. "He is a very quick shot which is why he always wins his duels."

"But you . . . ?" Zena asked in a whisper.

"I can only hope that I am swifter."

"What can I . . . say to you? It was . . . wrong of me . . . very . . . very wrong to ask your help . . . but when you . . . appeared at that very moment it seemed as if you had been sent by . . . God to help . . . us."

"Perhaps that is what happened," the *Comte* said with a smile. "When I heard you were coming to La Païva's tonight I obtained an invitation for myself, and whatever happens I am very glad I did so."

"Do you mean that?" Zena asked.

"Perhaps it is another way of proving how much you mean to me."

"If he . . . hurts you . . . I will never . . . forgive myself."

"Do not think of such things," the *Comte* admonished. "Believe instead that because what he was doing was wrong, overbearing and insulting, good will triumph over evil, and I shall be the victor."

"I shall pray. I shall be praying with my heart and soul," Zena said.

The *Comte*'s arms tightened around her, but he did not kiss her, and they drove in silence back to the Rue St. Honoré.

When they reached it the *Comte* obtained the key from the Concierge and took Zena to the bottom of the stairs.

When she expected him to climb up them with her he said instead:

"Go to sleep, my darling. Try to think of nothing but the happiness we shall enjoy together tomorrow when I show you the pictures in the Louvre."

Zena did not speak and the *Comte* went on:

"I am going back now to see that de Villerny gets into no more trouble and to arrange my seconds. After that I shall rest."

"How can I tell you how . . . wonderful you are to . . . me?" Zena asked.

"I hope that you will be able to do that tomorrow," the *Comte* replied.

He took both her hands, and raised them one

after the other to his lips. Then he said very quietly:

"Goodnight, my precious love. Sleep well, but remember me in your prayers."

The way he spoke brought the tears to Zena's eyes, but before she could answer or try to find words in which to express her feelings he disappeared through the outer door into the street.

Slowly she went up the stairs feeling as though when she had least expected it the roof had caved in and her dreamworld was in ruins about her feet.

# Chapter Five

Zena took off her ballgown and her evening slippers but did not undress any further.

She lay down on the bed waiting with the door open for Kendric to return.

She kept wondering how they could have got into such an impossible position as they were in now.

It seemed cruel and inexcusable that she should have involved the *Comte* to the point where he was fighting the *Marquis* to save Kendric without understanding why Kendric had to accept it.

The idea of Kendric being wounded and perhaps even killed in a duel in Paris was so horrifying that she found it difficult to think straight.

She was quite certain that if he fought a duel, even if he was victorious, somebody would become aware of who he was, and they would then have to explain not only to their father, but to the whole Court in Wiedenstein what they were doing in Paris.

Zena could not bear to think of what her mother would say if she ever learnt the part she was playing. She could only lie tense, praying fervently that everything would be all right, that Kendric would escape recognition and the *Comte* would not be hurt.

To know that he was fighting the most notoriously dangerous shot in France was an agony in itself.

Supposing he was killed? Supposing he survived, but never forgave her for involving him in such a perilous situation?

Then she remembered that anyway he would have to forget her, and although she could never forget him, once they had left Paris she would never see him again.

Everything was frightening, horrible and depressing to the point where Zena felt she must almost go insane because she could find no way out of their difficulties.

Slowly the hours dragged by and it was nearly four o'clock when at last she heard the outer door open and Kendric come into the Sitting-Room.

She jumped off the bed and ran to him saying as she did so:

"Why are you so late? What has happened?"

Kendric threw his hat and evening-cloak down on a chair, then put his arm around her shoulders to say:

"It is all right. Do not work yourself up, but I admit I am damned glad I am not to fight the *Marquis*."

"The *Comte* is doing it for you."

"I know that, and I am very grateful."

"I asked him to save you, and he did so."

"He is obviously very fond of you," Kendric said, "and I feel I am behaving very badly in letting him take my place. But what else could I do?"

He asked the question pathetically, almost as a small boy might have done.

"I have been thinking about that," Zena said. "I am certain that on no account could you fight the *Marquis*. Whether he wounded you or you wounded him, there would inevitably be a scandal about it. Then Papa would hear about us."

"You do not suppose I have not thought of that?" Kendric asked. "At the same time, to tell the truth I am ashamed of myself."

"I shall pray, I shall pray with all my heart that the duel will not be serious, then everybody will forget it ever happened."

Kendric did not answer and Zena was aware that he was not very optimistic.

He took his arm from her and walked towards his bedroom.

"I have to change," he said. "I am acting as a second for the *Comte* and as he did not seem to wish any of his own friends to be told about it, I have asked one of Philippe's, a man called Anton, to stand in."

"You are going to be with the *Comte!*" Zena said almost beneath her breath. "Then I am coming with you."

"You will do nothing of the sort," Kendric

replied. "Ladies never attend duels."

"I am attending this one," Zena said firmly. "How are you getting there?"

"In the carriage I engaged last night," Kendric replied. "I told the coachman to wait so that he could take us home from the party, and he is downstairs now, waiting again."

Kendric took off his evening-coat as he spoke and Zena sat down on his bed too.

"What I will do," she said, "is come with you and stay in the carriage. I shall be able to watch the duel, and then if we drive away immediately afterwards nobody will know I have been there."

"I have already told you that you are not coming," Kendric answered.

As he spoke he looked at his sister's face and said slowly:

"I suppose the worst has happened and you have fallen in love with the *Comte*."

It was inevitable, Zena thought, because they were so close to each other, that sooner or later Kendric would guess her feelings.

"I love him!" she said simply.

"Oh, God!" Kendric exclaimed. "That is all we want to make the whole situation completely impossible!"

"I cannot help it."

"Is he in love with you?"

"He says he is."

"Then swear to me on everything we hold holy that you will not tell him who we are," Kendric said. "I know he is a gentleman and I am sure he will behave like one, but you do realise that if inadvertently he revealed our secret to a friend, his valet, or anybody else, we could be black-mailed in a very unpleasant manner."

Zena was silent. Then she said:

"There is no point in my telling the *Comte* anyway. I realise that when we leave Paris I shall . . . never see him . . . again."

There was obviously a sob in her voice as she spoke the last words, and as if she was afraid of crying she ran from the room into her own.

She dressed hastily in the plainest of the gowns she had with her and covered it with a cloak that was of a dark green velvet and therefore not at all conspicuous.

She pulled the stars from her hair and because she still felt like crying washed her face in cold water before she went into the Sitting-Room.

Kendric was ready almost at the same time, and when he saw Zena's expression he put out his hand in a gesture of affection.

She took it in hers and he said as he drew her towards the door:

"Cheer up, dearest, things may not be as bad as we anticipate, and as we have both always known, one pays for one's fun in one way or another."

They walked down the stairs hand-in-hand and when they got into the carriage, Kendric directed the coachman to where they wished to go in the Bois.

It seemed as if the man knew the exact spot,

and Zena had the uncomfortable feeling that it would be impossible in Paris to keep a duel of any sort secret from the gossipmongers.

She did not say so to Kendric, but slipped her arm through his, feeling she needed the comfort of being close to him.

"The *Comte* will be all right," he said as if she had asked the question.

"What shall we . . . do if he is . . . wounded?" Zena asked.

"He has arranged for a doctor to be present, and doubtless the *Marquis* will do the same," Kendric said. "Whatever happens, they will both have proper medical attention."

'That would not be of much use,' Zena thought, 'if the *Comte* was killed.'

She knew, because her father had often discussed what happened in duels, and she had also read about them, that it was customary for the duel to be more a ritual of honour than anything else.

A very slight wound was considered satisfaction for the insult in most cases, and as far as aristocrats were concerned, it was considered both unsporting and ill-bred to injure a rival seriously.

But she did not trust the *Marquis* knowing instinctively that he was both evil and dangerous, and she had the terrifying feeling that he would do anything however outrageous to get his own way where she was concerned.

'If the *Comte* loses the duel,' she thought,

'Kendric and I will have to go home to . . . avoid him.'

It was agonising to think that she might have to leave the *Comte* even sooner than she had expected, and as the carriage drove towards the Bois she tried not to think about it.

When they reached the place, which was a small clearing in the middle of a wood, Zena could see in the dim light there were already some men standing about.

Dawn was just breaking and a few minutes ago the first rays of the sun had come up over the horizon.

"Now swear to me," Kendric admonished, "that you will make sure that nobody sees you. We shall be in worse trouble than we are already if anybody realises that I have brought you with me."

"You could not have stopped me," Zena replied.

He touched her shoulder gently, then he stepped out of the carriage and shut the door carefully behind him.

Zena watched him walk away, then with a leap of her heart she saw the *Comte* come through the trees on the other side of the clearing and meet Kendric.

There was another man with him whom Zena thought must be Anton and a few seconds later an elderly man carrying what was obviously a doctor's bag joined them.

It was difficult for her to take her eyes from the

*Comte* but she looked to where at the other end of the clearing the *Marquis* was talking to his two seconds and another doctor.

As the sky rapidly grew lighter she could now see them clearly, and she thought the *Marquis* looked particularly unpleasant and even more debauched than when he was at La Païva's house.

His eyes seemed dark and sinister and his lips were set in a cruel line, which convinced her that he was determined to injure the *Comte*.

Her eyes returned irresistibly to the man she loved and she found herself praying with a fervour which came from her heart and soul.

"Please . . . God . . . save him! Please . . . God let him . . . win. Do not let him be hurt. Please . . . God . . . help us."

She repeated the words over and over, feeling as if they were carried on wings into the sky and God who had given her love must understand and listen to her plea.

Nothing seemed to be happening and she wondered why they did not get on with the duel.

Then as another man appeared and walked into the clearing she understood that they had been waiting for the Referee.

He was much older than either of the contestants and looked extremely distinguished. He beckoned to them both and spoke to them for some seconds. Zena was certain he was admonishing them as to their behaviour.

Then the box containing the duelling-pistols

was opened, and as the *Marquis* considered he was the person who had been insulted he had the first choice of weapons.

Then obviously on the Referee's instructions the duellists walked into the centre of the clearing to stand back to back waiting for the contest to begin.

Both men were wearing smartly cut day-coats and top hats.

The *Comte*, Zena noticed, as she had yesterday when they had driven in the Bois, wore his hat at a somewhat raffish angle, and it gave her the impression that he was confident that he could defeat the *Marquis* despite the latter's reputation.

Because she was so afraid she intensified her prayers feeling that somehow she could give him extra support and extra strength, and perhaps intensify his skill in handling his weapon.

Then as if she could not bear the tension of only watching and not hearing what was happening, she let down the window and as she did so she could hear the Referee begin to count.

"One . . . two . . . three . . ."

As each number was called the two contestants moved a pace away from each other and went on walking.

"Four . . . five . . . six . . . seven . . . eight . . . nine . . . ten!"

At the last word the *Marquis* and the *Comte* turned and Zena thought she must close her eyes because she could not bear to see what happened.

Two shots rang out almost simultaneously, then as she looked only at the *Comte* she saw as the smoke came from his pistol that he staggered.

She could not control her fear any longer and flinging open the door of the carriage she ran towards him as swiftly as her feet could carry her, knowing that nothing and nobody should stop her from reaching the man she loved when he had been wounded.

Finding that the *Comte* was still on his feet when she reached him she flung her arms around him saying frantically:

"You are ... hurt! Oh, darling ... darling ... I cannot ... bear it!"

She thought the *Comte* looked at her in astonishment, then one arm went around her.

"What are you doing here?" he asked.

Before Zena could reply a voice said:

"Let me see, *Monsieur,* if the bullet penetrated your arm."

Zena gave a little cry of horror and moved away a little as the doctor began gently to inspect the *Comte*'s arm.

"The shot was a little wide," the *Comte* said.

"It was you, *Monsieur* who hit *le Marquis,*" the doctor replied.

For the first time Zena looked away from the *Comte*.

She could see three men bending over something on the ground, and she realised that it was the *Marquis.*

She drew in her breath, but before she could speak Kendric was beside her.

"I told you to stay in the carriage!" he said sharply.

"I thought the . . . *Comte* was . . . hit," Zena murmured, but Kendric was not listening.

"You were magnificent!" he said to the *Comte*. "I have never seen such a fast shot!"

"I have had quite a lot of practice," the *Comte* replied, "not at men but at game birds."

The doctor had pulled his coat from his shoulder and now Zena could see that the *Marquis*'s shot had passed through the sleeve of the coat and through his shirt leaving a long red weal across the surface of his arm.

It was bleeding but not badly, and the doctor bandaged it as she stood watching.

"I think you would do well to enquire as to the condition of *Monsieur le Marquis*," the *Comte* said to Kendric.

"I hope you have made it impossible for him to go on making a nuisance of himself," Kendric answered.

"Let us go and find out," Anton said beside him.

Kendric looked at Zena.

"I will take Zena home," the *Comte* said before Kendric could speak, "and perhaps you will follow in your own carriage."

The way he spoke was so decisive that Kendric after a moment's hesitation walked away with Anton.

The *Comte* thanked the doctor, gave him what seemed to Zena to be an enormous number of francs, and then with his coat slung over one shoulder he said:

"Shall we go? As you are well aware, you have no right to be here."

"I am . . . sorry," Zena said in a contrite tone. "I promised Kendric I would not leave the carriage . . . but when I saw you . . . stagger I could not . . . help it."

"I am glad I did not know you were watching me," the *Comte* said. "It was very brave and very touching of you to come."

The *Comte*'s carriage was waiting on the other side of the trees and Zena got in, choosing her position on the seat carefully so that she would not be on the side of his injured arm.

The carriage started off and as she looked at him pleadingly the *Comte* said:

"My darling, you look tired."

"How could I sleep when I knew you were in . . . danger?"

"I feel you were praying for me."

"Desperately . . . and my prayers were . . . answered. I am more . . . grateful than I can possibly . . . say."

She gave a little sigh, then she said anxiously:

"You do not think you will run a temperature and become feverish?"

"It is only a scratch," the *Comte* answered, "and to tell the truth now it is over I feel rather elated that I have managed to defeat a man with such a formidable reputation as a duellist."

"You were wonderful!"

"Perhaps I had an unfair advantage with your prayers and my love for you to support me," he said gently.

Zena made an inarticulate little sound and put her head against his shoulder.

"Look at me, my darling," the *Comte* said.

She raised her face obediently and he looked down at her in the light of the pale morning sun coming through the windows of the carriage.

"You are even more beautiful that I have ever seen you before, without all that paint and powder on your face," he said.

Zena gave a little start.

She remembered how she had washed in cold water before she left the apartment, and because she was so unused to cosmetics she had not remembered to mascara her eyelashes or redden her lips as she had done ever since she came to Paris.

"As you are now," the *Comte* went on, "you look very, very young, innocent and — untouched."

It was as if he was speaking to himself rather than to her.

Then as Zena was wondering what she could say in reply his lips found hers and he was kissing her gently and tenderly, without passion, but it was very marvellous.

He kissed her until the horses turned into the Rue St. Honoré and as he raised his head Zena said as if the words burst from her:

"I love . . . you! I love you until it is . . . difficult to think of . . . anything else but you in my . . . life."

"Just as I think of you," the *Comte* said, "and, my darling when I come back and fetch you at luncheontime we have to talk about our future together, for I know now I cannot live without you."

"Our . . . future," Zena stammered.

It was as if an icy cold hand suddenly clutched at her heart.

"We have to be together," the *Comte* said. "Although we have known each other only a very short while, you fill my heart until I know that nothing else is of any importance except you."

He kissed her again, and as he did so the horses came to a standstill. The footman got down to open the door and the *Comte* said:

"Do not worry about anything, my darling. Leave everything to me. Go to bed and sleep as I intend to do. I will fetch you at one o'clock and then we will discuss everything which concerns ourselves."

Zena gave him a smile, then as she saw he was about to follow her out of the carriage, she said:

"Please . . . stay where you are. You know as well as I do you should move your arm as little as possible until the . . . bleeding has . . . stopped."

"Are you taking care of me?" the *Comte* asked with a smile.

"It is . . . something I would . . . like to do."

Their eyes met and it was hard to look away.

Then quickly Zena got out of the carriage, and in case he should follow her she ran through the outer door without looking back.

Zena was fast asleep when she heard Kendric calling her.

It was difficult to come back to consciousness and she hoped that he would go away and she could go on sleeping.

Then she felt his hand on her shoulder.

"Wake up, Zena! Wake up!"

"What . . . is it?" she asked.

She was so sleepy that for a moment it was difficult even to focus her eyes. Then she saw he was standing beside her bed, dressed as he had been when they went to the duel.

"Wake up, Zena!" Kendric said insistently. "We have to leave here at once!"

"L . . . leave . . . where for?"

"For home!"

As if he had thrown cold water on her face Zena sat up abruptly and opened her eyes.

"What is wrong . . . what has . . . happened?"

"We have to leave Paris at once," Kendric said, "and if you hurry we can catch a train to Hoyes which leaves at eleven o'clock."

"But . . . we cannot go . . . why should we?"

Kendric sat down on the side of the bed and pulled off his top-hat.

"The Press are asking questions," he said, "and you know what they are like when they sense there is a story which might cause a sensation."

"You mean . . . they intend to . . . write about the . . . duel?"

"Not because it is an ordinary duel of which there are plenty," Kendric replied, "about one a day I should think, but this one, for the Press, is exceptional."

"Why? Why?" Zena asked.

"Because it really is news that the *Marquis* should have lost a duel, with a serious injury to his arm."

"How serious?" Zena asked.

"He will not have to have it amputated or anything like that," Kendric replied, "but the fact that he has been injured in a duel over a woman and lost it is the sort of story all Paris will enjoy, especially when they know the name of the woman."

Zena gave a little cry of horror.

"So . . . that is . . . what they are . . . trying to find . . . out!"

"Exactly!" Kendric replied. "They already know that you came to Paris with me, and that I am supposedly the *Vicomte* de Villerny."

"But Kendric, how can they have found that out?"

"How should I know. I expect the *Marquis* talked. He had a great deal more to drink after you left La Païva's house last night, and I heard him saying in a loud voice that he would not only fight the *Comte* but me, to make sure he got you."

141

Zena gave a little groan.

"It is . . . all my . . . fault."

"You cannot help looking as you do," Kendric said. "I suppose it is something we might have anticipated when we came to Paris."

"What can we . . . do to . . . prevent them from . . . finding out . . . who we are?" Zena asked in a frightened voice.

"There is only one thing we can do," Kendric answered, "and that is to disappear."

He paused before he said:

"If we stay it is quite obvious they will ferret out that I am not de Villerny, and if they start making enquiries in Wiedenstein there is always the chance that your extraordinary likeness to the Princess Marie-Thérèse will be noticed."

Zena gave an audible cry of horror and Kendric stood up.

"I have already told Renée to come upstairs and start packing for you," he said, "and I have also ordered a carriage. You have only an hour in which to be ready to leave for the station."

"But . . . Kendric . . . what can I do about . . . the *Comte?*" Zena asked.

"Forget him!" Kendric replied.

Zena started to dress as Renée quickly but not very skilfully packed her gowns in the trunk in which they had come.

"It is sad that you must leave us, *M'mselle,*" she said. "It has been a pleasure having you here."

"Thank you," Zena replied absent-mindedly. Then she added:

"Renée, will you do something for me?"

"Of course, *M'mselle*."

"When *Monsieur le Comte* comes to call for me as he has promised to do, will you hand him a letter?"

*"Oui, M'mselle."*

Zena at first thought it would be wisest to go away without making any explanation. Then she had known it was something she could not do.

She loved the *Comte* and he loved her.

Before she went to sleep she had thought despairingly it would be very difficult to listen to him trying to make plans for their future and not to confess the truth.

She thought that perhaps Fate had taken a hand, and to go away without explanation was better than having to lie.

At the same time, every instinct in her body which loved him told her she was being a fool.

But what could she say?

How could she confess there was no possibility of any future for them together and that their love was just something wonderful and glorious which had come into their lives for a fleeting moment.

When she was dressed for the journey and Renée was packing the last few things into her bag Zena ran into the Sitting-Room and taking some pieces of writing-paper and an envelope from the *Secretaire* carried them with her to her bedroom.

She had the feeling that if Kendric saw her writing he would think it a mistake and perhaps argue with her, which she could not bear.

Then as she sat down at her dressing-table and wrote the first words she heard his voice talking to Renée's father who had been helping him pack.

Quickly because there was now no time, she scribbled:

*"I love you, I love you! But I have got to go away. And yet because I must tell you how kind and wonderful you have been and that I shall never forget you, I will write to you once again when I reach my destination.*

*My Love and my Prayers,*
*Zena."*

As she finished and folded the letter into the envelope Kendric was at the door.

"Are you ready, Zena! We must go!"

"Everything is packed, *Monsieur*," Renée replied.

The maid diverted his attention from his sister and while he was giving instructions to the Concierge to carry the trunk downstairs Zena managed to give the letter to Renée and with it a ten-franc note.

Renée slipped both into the pocket of her apron.

144

*"Merci, M'mselle,"* she said in a voice that Kendric could hear. Then she added quietly: "I will not forget to do what you have asked, *M'mselle.*"

The luggage was piled on the roof of the carriage, and as they drove away down the Rue St. Honoré Zena looked up at the windows of the Sitting-Room.

She was thinking of how the *Comte* had kissed her and she had never guessed how perfect and glorious a kiss could be. She knew she would never forget the rapture and the ecstasy which had made her feel he carried her to the heart of the sun.

"How can I live and never know such happiness again?" she asked herself and felt as if the whole world was dark.

It took them nearly two hours to reach Hoyes and there they had to wait for the slow train to carry them on to Ettengen.

They had picked a compartment to themselves when they left Paris, but Zena had said very little to Kendric because he was tired after not being able to go to bed all night, and he soon fell asleep.

She too felt tired, but she could only think of the *Comte* and wonder what he would think and feel when Renée gave him her note and he learnt that she and Kendric had left Paris.

She remembered all the words of love he had ever spoken to her, and she knew that she would

145

repeat them and repeat them all her life and they would be her only comfort and help in the years of misery which lay ahead.

At Hoyes, Kendric, as if he needed exercise, began to walk up and down the platform.

Zena sat on the hard wooden seat feeling no impatience to continue their journey, but only a dull disinterest in everything that happened.

Finally the slow train from the capital arrived and Kendric found an empty first class carriage and Zena stepped into it.

Then as Kendric tipped the Porter the man said:

" 'Scuse me, *Monsieur,* but has anybody ever told you you've a striking resemblance to our Crown Prince?"

Kendric smiled.

"I believe I have heard that before."

"Uncanny it is, *Monsieur,* you might be almost his double."

"I will take that as a compliment," Kendric joked.

"He's a very fine young man, and we're exceedingly proud of him," the Porter said. "In time he'll make us a good ruler."

"I hope he does not disappoint you," Kendric remarked.

As the train moved off he said to Zena:

"It is always pleasant to receive an unsolicited testimonial. Do you think I will make a good Arch-Duke?"

"Not if you behave as you did in Paris!"

146

Kendric laughed.

"I suppose I should apologise to you. At the same time, I enjoyed myself, and it will be something to remember when I am at Düsseldorf."

The way he spoke made Zena realise again how much he was dreading the thought of a year under Prussian military authority.

She put out her hand to say:

"We must neither of us regret anything we have done, but just be glad that we were lucky enough to know such happiness."

The way she spoke made her brother aware how much she was suffering, and after a moment he said:

"If I were on the throne, I swear Zena, I would make it possible somehow for you to marry the *Comte* and live happily ever afterwards."

"Thank you, Kendric," Zena said, "but although it is an agony to know that I will . . . never see him again . . . I shall always be glad that I knew and loved such a . . . wonderful man . . . and he loved me."

Kendric sighed, and there was nothing he could say to comfort her.

After they had travelled for some miles in silence Kendric said:

"Do not forget we are now the *Comte* and *Comtesse* de Castelnaud."

"I had forgotten," Zena replied and wished she could continue to be Zena Bellefleur.

When they reached the Professor's house

which was on the outskirts of the small village of Ettengen, a tall red-brick ugly building which looked, Zena thought, rather like a School, they were both wondering what the Countess and the Baron had done about their disappearance.

"I can tell you one thing," Kendric said as they drove from the station in a hired carriage, "our watch-dogs, if they have not run tittle-tattling to Papa, will be waiting to bite us. So be prepared for a very uncomfortable reception."

He had not exaggerated and the only thing that mitigated the anger of those waiting for them was that they had arrived sooner than they had said they would.

When they walked into the house and were shown into the room where the Countess and the Baron were sitting with the Professor, the exclamations at their appearance and the re-criminations they received made it impossible for them for sometime to make any explanation.

Then at last with an authority which Zena thought Kendric had never shown before he said sharply:

"That is enough. My sister and I have not returned to be scolded as if we were school-children!"

He looked towards the Professor before he said:

"First, *Mein Herr*, I must apologise to you for not arriving when we were expected. But her Royal Highness and I have missed only a few days of our tuition, and we can easily make up

148

the time lost if we apply ourselves to our studies as we both intend to do."

Zena saw at once that the Professor was somewhat mollified, and thinking that Kendric had started off on the right foot she said:

"As I am tired after my journey, I should be grateful Herr Professor, if somebody could show me to my bedroom, and, if it is possible, I would like a cold drink. It was exceedingly hot in the train."

The Professor hurried to give the orders and the Countess with her affronted dignity showing itself with every word she spoke showed Zena upstairs to a quite pleasant room overlooking the garden at the back of the house.

"Your clothes have been unpacked, *Mademoiselle la Comtesse,*" she said, "but before I ring for the maid I would like to tell you . . ."

"I am very fatigued," Zena interrupted, "and as I have no wish to sit through a long-drawn-out dinner please have something brought to me on a tray."

The Countess was astounded.

"Your Royal — I mean *Mademoiselle la Comtesse,* must be ill!"

"Only tired," Zena said, "and please be so obliging as to give the orders for what I require . . ."

She thought as she spoke that if Paris had given Kendric a new authority it had made her feel as if she was no longer a child, but grown up.

"I am old enough to be loved," she told herself, "and that makes me a woman, and as a woman I will no longer be imposed upon by people who should obey my orders rather than I should obey theirs."

As a matter of fact she was definitely too tired to wish for arguments or to do anything but rest.

But there was one thing she knew she had to do first — for she would be unable to sleep otherwise — and that was to write again to the *Comte*.

She waited until she was in bed, then writing with a pencil instead of pen and ink she covered three pages of writing-paper with the expression of her love.

Finally she wrote:

*"You have given me something so priceless, so perfect, that it will shine like a light to guide me all through my life.*

*Although I can never see you again, and it breaks my heart to write this, I know, because I have loved you, I will become a far better person.*

*I think love — true love — makes those who find it want to be good, and to inspire others. That is what I shall try to do because you have inspired me and your love is like a guiding star.*

*It will be always out of reach, yet it will be there, shining in the Heavens above me, and I will follow it, as the Wise Men followed the Star of Bethlehem.*

*I know too that although you may not be aware of it, I shall sometimes be near you in my dreams, and my love will reach out to protect you as it did when you were fighting the Marquis.*

*There is nothing more I can say, nothing more I can tell you, except that now and for all eternity my heart and soul are yours.*

*Zena.*"

She did not read the letter through but put it straight into an envelope.

She knew that if she addressed it to: *Le Comte Jean de Graumont c/o Le Duc de Soissons, Les Champs Élysées, Paris,* the letter would find him.

She rang the bell and when the maid answered it she asked her if she would take the letter at once to the Post Office.

The maid who was German like the Professor looked at Zena a little doubtfully, and Zena said:

"As it is very important, if you will go at once, I will of course pay you for your services. Please give me my handbag."

She thought as she spoke that the woman's eyes glinted greedily, and when she drew a ten-franc note from her bag and handed it with the letter and another note of a smaller denomination with which to buy the stamp the servant curtsied.

"I will take it at once, *Mein Fräulein,*" she said in her gutteral voice. Then she added as if perceptively she guessed what Zena wanted to hear: "and no one will know I have left the house."

"Thank you," Zena said.

Then as if at last she was free to rest, she put her head down on the pillow and closed her eyes.

Just for a moment she wanted to cry for her lost love and for the *Comte,* wondering despairingly why she had left him.

Then instead she imagined his arms were around her, and he was holding her close, his lips seeking hers.

She felt her love rising within her and the happiness he had given her seemed to seep over her like sunshine.

Because it was so wonderful, so perfect, and she loved him so much, she fell asleep.

# Chapter Six

Zena walked slowly down the stairs to the Library.

They had now been four days at Ettengen and she felt as if four centuries had passed and that every day her yearning for the *Comte* grew more intense, more agonising.

She thought that perhaps at first she had been almost numbed by the shock of the duel, of leaving Paris in such a hurry, and being plunged into the intolerable boredom of the companionship of the Baron and the Countess.

Every night as she cried herself to sleep she thought she had lost the sunshine from her life, and she would never again know anything but darkness and misery.

Last night she had felt it was too heart-rending to bear any longer, and after they had all retired to bed she had gone to Kendric's room to tell him she must run away.

"It is no use, Kendric," she said, "I cannot face life without the *Comte* in fact I would rather be dead!"

"Things will get better as time goes by," Kendric said soothingly.

He was lying back against the pillows, in his bed reading a book, and now as he looked at his sister sitting on the mattress facing him he knew how deeply she was suffering.

He thought she was already beginning to look like Melanie although otherwise there was little resemblance in their appearance.

"I am sorry, Zena," he said impulsively, "I should never have taken you to Paris."

"I shall never regret it," Zena replied fiercely. "I would not have missed meeting the *Comte* for . . . anything in the world, but why should I . . . suffer like . . . this? Why should I marry a man I will . . . hate?"

She paused, then she said slowly and distinctly:

"I am going back to Paris to find the *Comte,* and as far as Wiedenstein is concerned, I am dead!"

Kendric put out his hand to take hers.

"Now listen to me, dearest. You will not be dead, but the *Comte* will."

Zena stiffened.

"What do you mean?" she asked.

"I mean that Papa will find out where you are and the *Comte* will either be put in prison on some trumped up charge, or, if they feel he is too important for that, he will have a 'regrettable accident'."

"I do not believe it!" Zena cried. "You are just trying to frighten me into not going back to Paris!"

Kendric's fingers tightened on hers.

"You know I want you to be happy," he said. "Do you remember our Cousin Gertrude?"

Zena thought for a moment.

"Do you mean . . . the one who is now the Queen of Albania?"

Kendric nodded.

"Yes. Like you, when she was told she had to marry a rather coarse, uncivilised King and live in Albania, she rebelled."

"What happened?" Zena asked in a low voice.

"Gertrude had fallen in love with one of the Diplomats at her father's Court. He was a Frenchman and as they loved each other passionately they felt the world was well lost for love."

"That is what I . . . feel," Zena said beneath her breath.

"They arranged to run away together and Gertrude made plans to creep out of the Palace and join him. They thought they would leave the country before anybody was aware of what was happening."

"Why were they . . . unable to . . . do so?" Zena asked.

Her voice was hardly above a whisper and her eyes were apprehensive.

"The day before they were due to leave, when they were quite certain that nobody had the slightest idea of their plans, the Diplomat went out riding as he did every morning, was thrown from his horse and broke his neck!"

There was a long silence. Then Zena said:

"Was it not really an accident?"

"He was an expert rider," Kendric replied, "and it is very unusual for any man to die if he is bucked off his horse or even thrown over its head."

There was another long silence. Then Zena said:

"And you think . . . something like . . . that might . . . happen to the . . . *Comte?*"

"I am certain of it," Kendric replied. "That way there would be no scandal, and nobody would know except Papa and Mama. You would be brought back, and the *Comte* would be dead."

Zena put her hands over her face and her brother knew that she was crying.

He put his arms around her and said:

"This is the penalty we both pay for being who we are, and you surely do not suppose that when the time comes I will be allowed to choose my own bride? I will have to marry some boring Princess who will be chosen for me, and I shall have to make the best of living with her, whatever she is like."

"At least you will be . . . able to get . . . away . . . sometimes," Zena said in a muffled voice.

"I hope so," Kendric replied.

He was thinking of how his father had said he would like to go to Paris but found it impossible.

Zena took her hands from her face and wiped her eyes.

"I will . . . try to be . . . brave," she said, "but it will be . . . worse when . . . you are not . . . here."

"It will be very much worse for me also!" Kendric said grimly.

They talked for a long time, but could find no way out of a future that was looming nearer every day that passed. For the moment the only mitigating factor was that they could suffer together.

When Zena went back to bed she had cried not only because she had lost the *Comte* but also because she must lose her twin.

As if in tune with her feelings the day had started misty and dull, but the sun had come out while they were working with the Professor in the room he called the Study. It made the lessons, which were excruciatingly dull, seem worse than they usually were.

The Professor was a perfectionist. He corrected every mispronunciation, every intonation, every grammatical mistake, until Zena felt she must scream.

What made the lessons even more intolerable was the fact that, because they had escaped their watch-dogs once, the Countess and the Baron sat in the Study all the time they were being taught.

They also accompanied them, as Kendric said angrily, every time they moved, in case they should run away again.

"It is our own fault," Zena told him listlessly,

and knew the only way she could escape now was in her thoughts.

When luncheon was over, a heavy German meal which was very unlike the French cuisine they had at the Palace, the Professor retired for a rest.

He was an old man and everyone knew that for two hours after luncheon he would sleep.

As they started their lessons quite early in the morning this seemed such an excellent idea to the Baron and the Countess that they too insisted on a *siesta,* and told Zena and Kendric they should do the same.

Because they were so frightened that their charges would vanish for a second time each day they extracted from them a promise on their word of honour that neither of them would leave the house or the garden.

"I am so relieved to get rid of the old crows I would promise to do anything!" Kendric said when their attendants had left them alone.

"I suppose they are only doing their duty," Zena replied, "and we certainly frightened them."

Kendric picked up the newspapers.

"It is too hot to stay in the house," he said. "I am going to read in the garden under the trees. Come and join me."

"I will in a minute," Zena replied. "But I must first find something to read."

"I do not think you will find much in the Professor's Library, except history books," Kendric scoffed.

Zena felt that even that would be better than having nothing to do but think, which inevitably led to her crying for the *Comte*.

Kendric picked up the newspapers and went off into the garden, while Zena went to the Professor's Study where the walls were lined with books.

She found some on one shelf which were in French, and she was taking them out one by one to see if there was anything she wanted to read, when the door opened behind her and she thought Kendric had come back.

"You were right!" she said. "Everything here is so unutterably dull."

"Perhaps you would prefer to talk to me," a man's voice said.

Zena started so violently that she almost dropped the book she was holding in her hands.

Then as she turned round she saw in amazement that it was the *Comte* who was standing inside the door.

He looked so handsome, so tall and elegant, that for a moment she thought she must be dreaming and she was seeing a vision of him as he had looked when he took her to luncheon in the Bois.

He shut the door behind him and came forward into the room.

It was impossible for Zena to move and she was holding her breath.

Then as she longed to run to him to touch him and make sure he was really there she said in a voice that trembled:

"W . . . what has . . . happened? Why are you . . . here?"

"I am here," the *Comte* replied with a smile, "because they informed me at the *Gendarmerie* that the only beautiful young woman in Ettengen with red-gold hair and blue eyes was the *Comtesse* de Castelnaud."

"You were . . . looking for . . . me?" Zena asked in a voice that did not sound like her own.

The *Comte* came nearer and when he reached her side he said:

"You have driven me nearly mad by disappearing in that cruel fashion and leaving me no address and no idea how I could find you."

"I told . . . you that I could never . . . see you again."

"I was in despair, utter and complete despair!" the *Comte* said, "in fact I have never been so unhappy in my whole life."

"But . . . you are . . . here."

"I am here," he repeated, "thanks to the second letter you wrote to me."

"I did not put any address on it," Zena said quickly.

"The Post Office did that for you," the *Comte* replied. "When I saw the letter was stamped 'Ettengen' I took the first train from Paris that would carry me to Wiedenstein."

Zena put down the book she was carrying as if it was too heavy to hold.

"So that is . . . how you . . . found me."

She could not help the lilt in her voice or the fact that her eyes were shining radiantly in her pale face.

"That is how I found you!" the *Comte* confirmed.

As he spoke he put his arms around her and drew her against him.

Zena felt her heart turn over in her breast and she lifted her face up to his.

He did not kiss her, he only looked down at her for a long moment before he said:

"I have found you, and now I want to know how soon you will marry me, for I have discovered, my darling, that I cannot live without you."

He pulled her almost roughly towards him, then his lips were on hers.

Now he kissed her in a very different way than he had done before. His lips were passionate and demanding, and there was a fire in them which told Zena that, because he had suffered, he could no longer control his feelings.

It flashed through her mind that if the first kiss she had received from him had been like this, she might have been frightened. But now something wild and wonderful within her leapt to meet the fire in him.

Once again he carried her into the sun, and the light of it seemed to blaze around them as she knew this was another side of love which was wonderful, exiting, demanding, and she gloried in it.

He kissed her until Zena felt her misery and

depression was swept away, and her whole body vibrated to a force that was stronger and more vital than anything she had ever known before.

She felt as if she had suddenly come alive, and no sensation she had ever known in the past had been so rapturous, so ecstatic as what the *Comte* was making her feel now.

His heart was beating tempestuously against her own and she knew the sensations he was giving her he was feeling himself, and it made them one person as truly as if they were married and nothing could divide them.

When at last the *Comte* raised his head Zena felt that if he were not holding her in his arms she would have fallen to the ground.

Because she was pulsating with emotion she could only hide her face against his shoulder and say in a breathless little voice:

"I . . . love you . . . I love . . . you and I thought I would . . . never see you again."

"And I love you!" the *Comte* said. "Never again my darling, will I lose you. Nothing shall prevent you from being mine."

He spoke with a violence that seemed to echo his kisses, and it was only with a superhuman effort that Zena remembered that what he was saying was impossible.

"I . . . I must talk to . . . you," she said.

The *Comte*'s lips were pressed against her forehead.

"What is there to talk about?" he asked. "I have learnt that you are not who you pretended to be, and the *Vicomte* de Villerny is really the *Comte* de Castelnaud."

Zena raised her face to look up at him.

"You . . . know who Kendric . . . is?"

"They told me at the *Gendarmerie* that he was your twin brother," the *Comte* smiled. "I was so overwhelmingly glad at the news that I would have given my informant several thousand francs if I had not been afraid of being arrested for bribery!"

He looked so happy as he spoke that Zena felt she could not bear to tell him the truth.

His arms tightened around her.

"How could you do anything so disgraceful as to come to Paris disguised in such a manner?" he asked. "I suppose I should be very angry with your brother for taking you to places where no lady should go, and letting you meet people who might have involved you in a great deal of trouble if I had not been there."

"But . . . you were . . . there," Zena said, "and you . . . saved me from the *Marquis*."

"If I had not been able to do so, I hate to think what would have happened," he said and his tone was grim.

"I was . . . always aware that I . . . could run . . . away," Zena said feeling she should make some explanation.

"You might not have been able to escape from the *Marquis* as easily as you escaped from me," the *Comte* said.

"I did not . . . want to . . . escape from . . .

you," Zena said in a whisper, "but Kendric said the Press were making 'enquiries' about us."

"I cannot help feeling you will get into a great deal of trouble if your parents, provided they are alive, discover your extremely improper masquerade," the *Comte* remarked.

The way he spoke told Zena now quite clearly that she must tell him who she was.

Just for a moment she played with the idea of persuading him to carry her away now, at this moment.

Perhaps they could find somewhere in the world where they could hide and where nobody would find them, where they could be together, and if his love was as great as hers nothing else would be of any consequence.

Then she remembered what Kendric had said last night and knew she loved him too much to risk his life, even though she might as well die without him.

The *Comte* put his fingers under her chin and turned her face up to his.

"You are so beautiful, so ridiculously, adoringly beautiful," he said. "How could you not expect in that ridiculous guise of pretending to be a *demi-mondaine* that every man who looked at you would not wish to possess you?"

Now there was a scolding note in his voice which she knew was because he had been frightened for her.

"It may . . . seem to you very . . . wrong," she said, "and perhaps . . . immodest . . . but if I had not . . . gone to Paris I would not have . . . met you."

There was a smile on the *Comte*'s lips as he said:

"That is a very plausible excuse, my precious one. At the same time it is something that can have a lot of unpleasant consequences in the future."

Seeing she did not understand he explained:

"I shall not be able to take you to Paris again, until not only the Prince Napoleon has forgotten what you look like but also the *Marquis* de Sade."

"That would not . . . matter to . . . me if I could be . . . anywhere else with you," Zena said, "but . . . there is something I must . . . tell you."

Her voice trembled and the *Comte* looked at her searchingly.

"What is wrong?" he asked. "I love you, and I know that you love me. All I want, my precious, beautiful little Wiedensteiner, is that we should be married, and as quickly as possible."

"What is . . . what I have to . . . tell you," Zena said. "I . . . cannot marry you."

"Why not?"

The *Comte*'s voice was sharp and seemed to ring out.

Because she felt she could not bear to wipe away the love from his eyes or the smile from his lips Zena gave a little cry and said:

"Before I tell you, will you . . . kiss me once . . . again as you did . . . just now?"

"You are making me nervous," the *Comte* complained. "Now I have found you nothing matters except that to love you and look after you, and above all prevent you from doing dangerous and unpredictable things like pretending to be a *demi-mondaine!*"

The smile was back on his lips as he said:

"I think I felt from the first moment I looked at you that your darkened eyelashes and red lips were wrong, and when I talked to you I realised quickly how innocent you were, unless of course you were the most brilliant actress who ever performed on any stage."

"Did you really . . . think that?" Zena asked. "And it did not . . . shock you?"

"I was very shocked that you should have been to that low Dance-Hall in Montmartre and that you agreed to have luncheon alone with a stranger in the Bois."

He paused and Zena said in a voice he could hardly hear:

"I . . . I did not mean to let you . . . kiss me . . . but it was . . . so wonderful . . . so perfect that I cannot . . . believe even now that it was . . . wrong."

"It was the first time you had ever been kissed?" the *Comte* asked.

"Y . . . yes."

"I knew it!" he exclaimed. "I knew when my lips touched yours that they confirmed what I had already thought, that you were pure and innocent."

"I am . . . glad you thought . . . that."

"At the same time it is certainly something which must never happen again," the *Comte* said, "and it never will when I am looking after you."

His words brought back to Zena's mind what she had to tell him and because she was afraid she felt herself trembling.

"What is upsetting you?" he asked. "Tell me, my darling, and let us get it over. Then we can make plans for our future."

It was what he had said before, and she remembered when she left Paris she had known there was no future with him.

Then as the tears would have swept over her in a floodtide she shut her eyes.

"Kiss me . . . please kiss me," she pleaded, "then I will tell you . . . what you . . . have to know."

The *Comte* held her so closely against him that she could hardly breathe. Then he kissed her at first gently, then compellingly and possessively.

He took his lips from hers to kiss her eyes, her nose, then the softness of her neck beneath her ear.

She was surprised he should do so and she felt rising within her a strange and exciting feeling which was different from anything she had ever felt before.

It made her feel wild and for some reason she could not understand it was hard to breathe, and when she did, her breath came in little gasps from between her parted lips.

Once again the *Comte* kissed her lips, and she wished she could die before she must tell him who she was, and know they must say goodbye again.

When finally he released her, her cheeks were flushed, her lips were red from his kisses and her eyes seemed to hold all the sunlight in them.

"I . . . love . . . you . . . Jean."

It was the first time she had ever used his Christian name and somehow it made her feel as if she belonged to him so completely that there were no titles or rank to divide them.

They were just a man and a woman in love — Zena and Jean.

He looked down at her and there was a smile of triumph on his lips as if he felt he had won a battle and the enemy had surrendered.

"Now tell me what you have to say," he said.

As if she could not bear to do so while he was touching her, Zena moved away from him to stand at the window looking out into the garden.

She did not see the sunshine, the trees, the flowers, or Kendric in the distance lying on the grass reading the newspapers.

Instead she only saw the grandeur of the Palace, the Throne Room where her father and mother sat on official occasions and the smaller chairs on either side of them which were also ornate and rather like thrones for Kendric and herself.

She must have stood silent for several seconds

before the *Comte* said:

"I am waiting!"

"I . . . I . . ."

Zena's voice seemed to come from a very long way away and be almost inarticulate.

"I am not . . . who you . . . think I . . . am."

"Not the *Comtesse* de Casteluaud?"

"N . . . no."

"Another disguise?" the *Comte* asked.

Zena nodded.

"Then who are you?" he asked. "Let me say before you tell me, that whoever you are — Zena Bellefleur or *La Comte*sse de Casteluaud or whoever else — to me you are the woman I love and whom I will make my wife."

"If only . . . I . . . could be . . . married to you, I would be the . . . happiest person in the . . . whole world."

The way she spoke was so poignant that even the *Comte* was startled.

"Why can you not marry me?" he asked. "You cannot be married already?"

"N . . . not . . . exactly."

"Then if you are engaged," the *Comte* replied, "forget it! I suppose, as in all French families, you have been affianced to some suitable young man by your parents and you have no choice in the matter. Then let me make it clear before we go any further — you will marry me!"

Once again Zena wondered if she should agree to do as he wished, on condition that he took her away immediately.

She was sure she could persuade Kendric to help them, and it could actually be quite easy to escape from the house at night, climb over the garden-wall and be over the border into France long before dawn.

It might take them a week or longer to find out that it was the *Comte* who had spirited her away and by that time they would be married and legally she would be his wife.

'That is what we will do,' she thought. 'I will pretend that all I was going to tell him was that I am engaged.'

As this was going round in her head she remembered Cousin Gertrude and what had happened to the man she had loved.

Would this be different? Zena knew she dare not risk it, and she must tell the *Comte* the truth.

As if he was reading her thoughts, which he had told her before he could do, he said:

"You must tell me the truth, Zena, however difficult it may be. To have secrets from each other would spoil our love and raise reserves and barriers between us."

Zena knew he was right.

However hurtful it might be for her, he must know the truth, and she could not sacrifice him to her love, however great it might be.

She took a deep breath. Then she said, slowly and in a voice that trembled on every word:

"I . . . am the . . . Princess Marie-Thérèse . . . of Wiedenstein!"

There was a long silence.

Zena felt the tears come into her eyes and she clasped her hands together so tightly that she squeezed the blood from her fingers.

"Is this true?" the *Comte* asked at length.

Zena was unable to speak, but she nodded her head.

"And as the daughter of the Ruler of this country you dared to go to Paris pretending to be a loose woman of a kind you should know nothing about?"

"K . . . Kendric was . . . upset and . . . unhappy," Zena said, "because . . . Papa had told him that he is to go to Düsseldorf for a year to train with the Prussian Cadets."

"I can understand his resenting that!" the *Comte* agreed. "But if he decided to go to Paris, how could he have dared to take you?"

"We have always . . . done everything . . . together," Zena answered, "so it would have been very . . . cruel of him to . . . leave me behind."

"He could have taken you as his sister."

"If he had done so he thought it would prevent him from enjoying himself because I would have to be chaperoned. So I . . . became his . . . *Chère Amie*."

"I can follow his thinking," the *Comte* said. "At the same time it was a mad, crazy idea from the start, and I cannot understand what your attendants did when you had run away."

"We managed it because we were coming here," Zena said. "The Paris Express stopped at

Hoyes while our train was in the station. We jumped into it leaving a . . . letter for the two . . . old people . . . escorting us telling them that if they told . . . Papa we had . . . disappeared he would be very . . . angry with them."

"It was quite ingenious, I admit," the *Comte* said, "but now the day of reckoning has come, Zena, what do you intend to do about us?"

Zena turned from the window.

"I want to marry . . . you," she said, "I would . . . give up my . . . hope of Heaven to be your . . . wife, to live with you and . . . love you. But it is . . . something that I . . . cannot do."

"Why not?" the *Comte* asked. "Is the pomp and circumstance of being Royal more important to you than our love?"

Zena walked towards him and put her two hands flat on his chest.

He did not put his arms around her, and she thought the way he looked at her was cold and critical.

"I love . . . you and I . . . swear to you I . . . love you more than . . . life itself," she said, "and if you were to marry me . . . I would go with you . . . anywhere in the . . . world."

"But it is something you will not do because you are a Royal Princess!"

"I want to . . . do it," Zena answered, "and if in order to hide we could only live in a hut I would . . . wait on you and . . . love you . . . and nothing else would . . . matter."

"And yet you still intend to send me away?"

172

"I have . . . to."

Her voice broke on the words.

"Why?"

She thought now there was a definite hardness in his eye. Because she had to make him understand she looked up at him pleadingly before she answered:

"Last night I told Kendric I could not . . . bear losing you . . . and I intended to run away . . . to go . . . back to Paris to . . . find you."

"But Kendric, very sensibly, persuaded you against it," the *Comte* said.

"He told me that if I did so," Zena replied, "you would . . . die!"

She felt the *Comte*'s body stiffen against her fingers.

"Why should he say that?"

"Because that had happened to one of our cousins. She was in love with a Diplomat but was told she had to . . . marry the King of Albania."

"What did she do?" the *Comte* asked.

"She was going to run away with the Diplomat, and they thought nobody knew about it. But he had what was called 'an unfortunate accident' when he was out riding and was found with a . . . broken neck!"

"And you think that kind of thing might happen to me?"

"Kendric is . . . sure of it, or else if you are not of . . . great importance you would be . . . imprisoned on some trumped up charge . . . perhaps for spying."

"In which case I would be shot," the *Comte* said reflectively.

Zena gave a little cry.

"How could I . . . allow it . . . how could I be . . . responsible for . . . that?"

She felt somehow that he was not convinced and she said:

"I love you! I love you so . . . desperately that if there were no . . . danger for you, I would pack my things and come away with you . . . now. But if we did that and you died, I would . . . kill myself!"

The last words were very low, but the *Comte* heard them.

It was then he put his arms around her and as he did so Zena burst into tears.

"I love you . . . I love you," she cried. "To be without you is like having a . . . thousand knives . . . driven into . . . my heart! But what . . . can I do? I cannot live . . . without you . . . but I cannot let you . . . die for my . . . sake!"

The tears became a tempest and now she sobbed despairingly against the *Comte*'s shoulder.

His arms tightened, they were very comforting and she felt his lips on her hair.

"Do not cry, my beautiful one," he said. "Our love should be happy and even though we met in extremely reprehensible circumstances I would not wish you to regret it."

"I do not . . . regret it! It was the most . . . wonderful thing that ever . . . happened to me," Zena sobbed, "but you might have been . . . injured or killed by the *Marquis* and now we have to say . . . goodbye to each other . . . and in a way . . . everything is my . . . fault."

"I think we should rather blame Fate," the *Comte* said. "Fate made you and your brother brave enough to run away, Fate put us next to each other at the Artists' Ball, Fate made me able to find you after I thought I had lost you for ever."

"But you . . . still have to . . . leave me."

She looked up at him as she spoke and he thought that even with the tears running down her cheeks and her lips trembling she was still the most beautiful person he had ever seen.

"I love you!" he said. "God, how I love you, but you have to be brave, my precious one."

"It is . . . not going to be . . . easy," Zena said, "and there is . . . something else I have not . . . told you."

"What is that?" he asked.

"Papa and Mama have arranged my marriage."

The *Comte* was still, then he asked:

"You are to be married — to whom?"

"To an . . . Englishman!"

"Does that horrify you?"

"Of course it . . . does! The English are . . . cold, arrogant and insensitive, and I shall have to live among . . . people who never laugh . . . without love and . . . without . . . you."

"And who is this Englishman?"

"His name is the Duke of Faverstone, and he

is coming to stay for the *Prix d'Or.*"

She thought the *Comte* did not understand and added.

"It is our most important race-meeting."

"I have heard of it," the *Comte* said. "But why should you marry an English Duke?"

"Because there are no Royal Princes available, and he is a relative of Queen Victoria."

"And you think you will be unhappy with him?"

"How could I be . . . anything else?" Zena asked. "Especially . . . now that I have . . . met you."

She gave a deep sigh.

"My sister Melanie is desperately miserable with the Crown Prince of Fürstenburg, and I shall be the . . . same."

The *Comte* was silent. Then he said very quietly:

"Then as I cannot bear to see you unhappy I shall have to save you, my darling."

"Save me?" Zena asked with an eagerness and for a moment there was a light in her eye.

Then she said, and her voice was dull again:

"There is . . . nothing you can do. Kendric was not speaking . . . lightly, and I know Papa would never . . . tolerate the scandal of my . . . running away so I would always be afraid that something . . . terrible would happen to you."

"Are you really thinking of me?" the *Comte* asked. "Or do you think life with your Duke in England would be preferable."

He did not wait for Zena to reply but went on:

"As you say, if we went into hiding, you and I might be very poor. Could love really mean enough to a woman to make her willingly give up her beautiful gowns, her jewellery, the comfort of having a lot of servants, just for one man?"

"I would wear rags . . . scrub floors and . . . beg for our food if I . . . could be with you."

Because there was a note in Zena's voice that had not been there before the *Comte* looked at her for a long moment before he pulled her against him and kissed her.

When once again she was pulsating with the wonder and rapture of his kiss, he said:

"I am going to find a way out of the *impasse* and it may not be as frightening as you anticipate it will be."

"You mean . . . I can be with . . . you?" Zena asked.

"I mean that I intend to marry you," the *Comte* said. "It is the first time — this is the truth, Zena — I have ever asked a woman to be my wife, the first time I have ever found a woman I knew I would be happy with for the rest of my life."

"As I would be . . . happy with . . . you."

"I will make sure of that by making you love me until no other man will ever matter to you."

"No other . . . man ever . . . will."

As Zena spoke she thought of the Duke and shivered.

Then in a voice that sounded desperate she asked:

"What can we do . . . what can we . . . do?"

"I have asked you to leave that to me," the *Comte* said, "and because I want to be sure of success I prefer not to talk about it."

"But . . . supposing you . . . fail?"

"Will it sound very conceited if I say I never fail in getting what I want in life?" the *Comte* replied. "And I want you, Zena, as I have never wanted anything else."

"I shall pray . . . I shall pray . . . desperately . . . as I prayed . . . before the duel," Zena said. "At the same time . . . I am . . . frightened."

"I am frightened too that I may lose you," the *Comte* said, "and now that you have told me who you are, perhaps I should leave."

Zena flung her arms around him.

"How can I let you . . . go?" she asked. "Supposing I never . . . see you again? I cannot . . . imagine what I would do! Oh, dearest, dearest Jean, I cannot lose you!"

"Nor I you," the *Comte* said. "That is why, my precious, you have to trust and believe in me."

"I know already that you are the most wonderful man in the whole world," Zena cried, "but it is still a question of Papa and the whole might of the Palace and the country which is involved. How can you . . . defeat all of them?"

"Love conquers all," the *Comte* said softly, "and we must believe that our love is big enough to do so."

"Mine is . . . I swear to you, mine is!" Zena said. "I love you until you fill the whole world.

There is no sky, no sea, sun, moon, or stars. There is only . . . you."

The *Comte* put his cheek against hers.

"I adore you!" he said. "One day I will be able to tell you how much. Then we will be married."

"If . . . only I could . . . believe you."

"Half the battle is always to believe that you will win," the *Comte* said. "So I am asking you, Zena, to believe in me."

Zena drew in her breath.

"I do . . . and I . . . will."

"Then we will win, my lovely one."

She could not reply for the *Comte* was kissing her again, kissing her until the rapture he always aroused in her swept through her and she knew that there was no need for words to tell him that she believed in him.

If her logical mind was still unconvinced she believed with her heart, her soul, her body, and her faith in God.

It was God who had brought them love and she knew indisputably that God would somehow make their dreams come true.

# Chapter Seven

As the train left Hoyes it began to gather speed towards the Capital.

Zena looked across the carriage at Kendric and knew that he was as apprehensive as she was.

When yesterday a Courier had arrived from the Palace to say they were to return immediately, they could only guess at the reason for their father's command and were both much alarmed by it.

As soon as she could be alone with Kendric Zena asked:

"Do you think Papa has found out that we went to Paris? Who could have told him?"

"God knows, but that may not be the reason he has sent for us."

"Then why should he want us back in such a hurry?"

"I cannot think," Kendric said.

It was then that Zena told her twin the secret she had kept from him for two days, that the *Comte* had been to see her.

"He came here?" Kendric exclaimed incredulously.

Zena nodded.

She went on to say that she had told the *Comte* the truth as to who she was and he had said whatever the obstacles, whatever the difficulties, he would marry her.

"You must be crazy if you believe him," Kendric said sharply.

"He told me to believe in him," Zena replied unhappily.

Kendric put his arm around her shoulder.

"Listen, Zena, I know what you are feeling, I know how unhappy you are, but I do not want you to have false hopes. They will only leave you more miserable than you are already."

"I love him!" Zena said. "Oh, Kendric, I love him so desperately."

"I know you do," Kendric answered soothingly, "but believe me when I tell you there is nothing you can do. If the *Comte* approaches Papa as a suitor for your hand, he will find himself in a great deal of trouble."

"I warned him of . . . that."

"Then if he is wise he will listen and go back to Paris," Kendric said. "I only wish I could do the same thing."

"So do . . . I," Zena murmured, and her voice broke on a sob.

The train reached the Capital late in the afternoon, and when Zena saw the Lord-in-Waiting on the station and a number of the Palace servants to attend to their luggage she felt as if the prison-gates of protocol and pomposity were waiting to close behind her.

Now she was no longer *la Comtesse* de Castelnaud, but Her Royal Highness Princess Marie-Thérèse.

They were escorted to their carriage by a number of the Railway Officials and drove away watched by a crowd which had assembled when they saw the Royal carriages.

As soon as she had the opportunity Zena said to the Lord-in-Waiting:

"Why has Papa sent for us? We did not expect to return for another ten days."

"I think His Royal Highness will wish to explain that to you himself," the Lord-in-Waiting replied, "but Your Royal Highness I am to ask you and Prince Kendric as soon as you arrive at the Palace to go straight to your rooms to change your clothes."

Zena looked surprised and the Lord-in-Waiting explained:

"Their Royal Highnesses are entertaining guests and you will find them in the Red Drawing-Room."

Hearing that was where they were to meet, Zena knew that the guests were of some importance and wondered which of their neighbouring Rulers was being entertained and if there was any particular significance in their visit.

Because she knew it was useless to ask questions she kept silent and concentrated on acknowledging those who waved to her from the sides of the road as they passed by.

"What do you think is happening?" she asked

Kendric in a low voice as they went up the stairs of the Palace side by side.

"I have no idea," he replied. "But I am thankful for anything which delays the storm which I fancy will break over our heads at any moment."

Because Zena felt frightened she changed her clothes as quickly as possible, paying little attention to the gown her maid chose for her to wear.

It was in fact a very pretty one, not so elaborate as those she had taken with her to Paris, but because it was more simple it made her look very young and spring-like.

Kendric came to her room to tell her he was ready, and feeling rather like schoolchildren who had been caught out playing truant they went down the stairs together and a footman opened the door of the Red Drawing-Room for them.

They entered to find there were quite a number of people with their father and mother.

The Arch-Duke detached himself to walk towards them as they approached and Zena lifted her face to kiss him.

"We are home, Papa!"

"I am delighted to see you, my dear!" the Arch-Duke replied.

The tone of his voice and the expression in his eyes made Zena know that their fears were unfounded, and whatever the reason they had been summoned back to the Palace, it was not because he was angry.

"How are you, my boy?" he asked Kendric.

"Very glad to be home, Sir," Kendric replied.

The Arch-Duke smiled as if he understood that his son had found Professor Schwarz extremely boring.

He then took Zena's hand in his.

"I brought you home," he said, "because the Duke of Faverstone has arrived sooner than we expected. He is talking to your mother, and I will present him to you."

Zena felt herself stiffen but there was nothing she could do but move beside her father through a crowd of Statesmen and politicians to where in front of the mantelpiece she could see her mother talking earnestly to somebody.

It was then she knew that Kendric was right and the *Comte* had talked nonsense when he said he would somehow make her his wife.

She felt the little glimmer of hope that had been in her heart since he had come to Ettengen flicker away as if it was candlelight that had been snuffed out by a heavy hand.

She was lost and nobody, not even the *Comte* could save her from an Englishman and England.

For one despairing moment she felt like running away and refusing to meet the Duke.

She could almost feel her feet carrying her towards the door and she knew the consternation such an action would cause.

But all the years of discipline in doing the right thing made her walk on beside her father until he stopped and she knew this was the moment

184

when her fate was sealed, and the man she loved had failed.

She wished the floor would open up and swallow her, she wished she could die.

Nevertheless she stood there stiff and tense, and because she dared not look at the man she was forced to take as a husband, she could not raise her eyes.

"So here you are, Zena!" she heard her mother's voice say.

Then a reply was unnecessary because her father interposed before the Arch-Duchess had even finished speaking by saying:

"Let me present, Zena, the Duke of Faverstone, who is an unexpected but very welcome guest."

Automatically Zena put out her hand.

She felt it taken in a strong grasp, and a deep voice said:

"I am enchanted to meet Your Royal Highness!"

There was something familiar in the tone and the fingers holding hers seemed somehow significant.

Slowly, as if she was compelled to do so, Zena raised her eyes.

Then she knew that she was either dreaming or had gone mad.

It was Jean she was looking at, Jean tall, dark and handsome with a smile on his lips and his eyes looking into hers with an expression of love which only she would understand.

For a moment she felt as if she had stopped breathing.

Then because it was so incredible and overwhelming she felt as if everything swam dizzily round her and she must faint.

With his hand still holding hers firmly, he said almost beneath his breath, and yet she heard:

"I told you to believe in me."

The platform was covered with a red carpet and the Royal Train gleaming white and red with new paint was waiting.

The applause of the crowd which had been deafening all the way from the Palace to the station could still be heard as the Royal Party accompanied the bride and bridegroom to the train.

Outside the door leading onto the platform Princess Marie-Thérèse, Duchess of Faverstone and her husband started to say goodbye to their relatives and the other Royal guests who were waiting to see them off on their honeymoon.

They were 'going away' much later than was usual because they had stayed for the Royal Banquet which had followed the marriage.

The Banquet should have taken place according to custom on the previous evening, but the Duke's horse had won the *Prix d'Or* on that afternoon and as was traditional he was the guest of honour at the Jockey Club Dinner which was always held after the race-meeting.

It had been anticipated that this might happen

and therefore the Banquet which had to be held while the visiting Royalty was still in the Capital had been postponed to the next evening.

It had been a long day of ceremony, and yet Zena was not tired.

She was so happy, so excited and thrilled that she felt as if she was flying on wings of ecstasy, and it was all part of a rapturous dream.

She had hardly had a chance of being alone with the Duke since she had discovered that he was the *Comte*.

She had a thousand questions to ask him once they could be together and not feel they were being chaperoned and watched so that it was difficult to talk about anything but commonplace subjects which could be safely overheard.

The Duke had spent two nights in the Palace after she had learnt who he was before returning to England to inform the Queen and his other relatives of their engagement.

They had actually been allowed only five minutes alone in which he was supposed to ask her formally to marry him.

How could they spend those few precious seconds talking when he could be kissing her?

"Is it true . . . is it really . . . true that you are the . . . Duke of Faverstone?" Zena managed to gasp disbelievingly as he took his lips for one second from hers.

"I asked myself very much the same question when Zena Castelnaud told me she was the Princess Marie-Thérèse," he replied.

Then he was kissing her again and explanations were unnecessary.

As Kendric said goodbye to his sister he said in a mischievous whisper that only she could hear:

"I bet you are thanking your lucky stars that you came with me to Paris!"

"I shall always be very, very grateful to you for thinking of such a reprehensible escapade," Zena replied.

The twins smiled at each other and Zena was grateful that Kendric was happy too.

The evening they had arrived back from Ettengen, when the guests in the Red Drawing-Room were proceeding upstairs to change for dinner, the Arch-Duke had said to him:

"By the way, Kendric, our plans have changed. You are not to go to Düsseldorf after all!"

Kendric had looked at his father hopefully.

"The Minister of Defence thinks that Germany is determined sooner or later to invade France, and it is essential for us not to appear to give Bismarck any encouragement."

"I certainly agree with that, Papa!" Kendric said.

"What we have therefore decided," the Arch-Duke went on as if he had not spoken, "is that we should send a Military Mission under General Nieheims to visit England and various countries in Europe, and you will accompany the General."

He saw the excitement in his son's face and

there was a smile on his lips as the Arch-Duke added:

"I think you will be glad to hear that the General's first visit will be to Paris."

"That is marvellous news, Papa!" Kendric exclaimed.

The Arch-Duke put his hand on his son's shoulder.

"I knew that would please you, and I wish I could come too."

"Perhaps it would be a good idea, Sir, if you joined me while I am there, to see how I am behaving on such an important mission."

The Arch-Duke laughed.

"I see, Kendric, you already have the makings of a Diplomat. I shall certainly consider your suggestion."

Father and son smiled at each other in conspiratorial fashion, then Kendric ran up the stairs to burst into Zena's bedroom to tell her his good news.

Because they had both been so happy they hugged each other as they had done when they were children.

"Will you see Yvonne in Paris?" Zena asked.

"I may set my sights somewhat higher," Kendric answered.

"But I am sure you will not be able to afford jewels from Massin's," Zena said and they both laughed.

Now after Zena had said goodbye to Kendric she kissed her mother, then her father.

"I wish you every happiness, my dearest," the Arch-Duke said.

"I am already happier than I have ever been in my whole life, Papa!" Zena replied.

He looked a little surprised, but her answer pleased him.

He supposed there was no point in saying so, but he had always bitterly regretted that his oldest child had been obliged to marry a man she disliked and who had made her so unhappy.

But there was no doubt as the train moved out of the station and Zena waved goodbye from the windows of the Saloon that her eyes were shining, and there was a radiance about her that seemed somehow to have transmitted itself to her bridegroom.

When the Royal Party was out of sight Zena turned to look at the Duke.

Their eyes met and she felt as if she was already in his arms.

Then he said without touching her:

"You have had a very long day, my darling. I suggest you go to bed, while I rid myself of this finery."

Zena gave a little laugh.

"You look very magnificent."

The Duke was wearing the uniform of a Colonel-in-Chief of the Royal Horseguards, his chest ablaze with decorations which Zena knew when they had time she must ask him to explain to her.

She thought it was impossible for any man to

look more magnificent, more distinguished or more lovable.

"I am not going to tell you what you look like until later," the Duke was saying. "It is however, something I am longing to do, so I beg you to hurry."

She gave him a little smile and moved across the Saloon towards the bedroom coach which it adjoined.

Zena knew the train well because her father always used it when he travelled not only in Wiedenstein, but to neighbouring Kingdoms and other parts of the Empire.

But she had never slept, of course, in the main bedroom which had been redecorated in time for her wedding.

It was the Duke who thought up the plausible excuse that they must be married with such unprecedented speed because his mother was in ill-health. If she died he would be in mourning and unable to marry for a year.

Zena was to find when she reached England that while her mother-in-law was under her Doctor's supervision, she was not on the danger list. In fact it was anticipated that she had many years of useful life in front of her.

Everyone in Wiedenstein was galvanised into immediate action by the Duke's insistence.

Zena watched the Duke's horse win the *Prix d'Or* then married him the next day and the whole country was wildly excited with the speed and thrill of it all.

At first her father and even more her mother had disapproved of what they called 'this very unseemly haste'. But that morning as Zena drove beside him in the State Coach to the Cathedral the Arch-Duke had said:

"If you ask me, it has done the whole of Wiedenstein good to be shaken out of their usual lazy lethargy by your wedding."

Zena turned her head for a moment to look at her father.

"Do you mean that, Papa?"

"I do," the Arch-Duke replied, "and because they have had to hustle and bustle to put up the decorations and to accommodate the huge crowds that have come into the Capital, I think we as a country have entered a new era of increased productivity."

Zena drew in her breath.

"It is all due to Jean," she wanted to say or rather 'John' as she was now told to call him.

Then she thought he could not take all the credit, only love could do that.

Now, as she entered the State Bedroom which had gold and white walls and blue sink curtains which matched her eyes, she felt like blushing.

The bed seemed to fill the small compartment, and as the lady's-maid took off her tiara and removed the glittering silver and diamanté gown she had worn for the Banquet, Zena's eyes kept straying to the lace-trimmed pillows bearing the Royal Insignia.

She was thinking she was glad they were to

spend tonight in the train instead of in the *Duc* de Soisson's Chateau which had been lent to them for their honeymoon in France.

At the Chateau, although they would be alone, there would be servants to wait on them, and inevitably when they arrived there would be a long line of officials and staff to be presented.

But tonight there was only a lady's-maid for her and a valet for the Duke and when they had retired to the coach where the other servants slept, she would be alone with her husband.

Zena knew too that the train was travelling for only a short distance before it stopped in a siding for the night.

Then there would be no rumble of wheels to prevent her from hearing the words of love which she knew the Duke was longing to say to her, just as she had so much to say to him.

Wearing a diaphanous nightgown of chiffon trimmed with lace which had come from Paris, and which the Arch-Duchess had said she considered extremely immodest, Zena got into bed.

It was very soft and comfortable and the sheets felt cool after the heat of the day.

The maid picked up her gown and looked around to see that everything was tidy before she curtsied.

"*Bon soir*, Your Royal Highness!"

"*Bon soir*, Louise," Zena replied.

Now she was alone, and there was only one shaded light left by the side of the bed.

She waited, her heart beating frantically in her

breast, as the door opened and the Duke came in.

She felt as if he was enveloped with light as he had been when she had seen him standing against the sunshine in the Sitting-Room in the Rue St. Honoré.

She knew now that it was the light of love which seemed to burn through them both.

With her red-gold hair falling over her shoulders, her blue eyes very wide and shining in her small face, the Duke thought it was impossible for anybody to look lovelier, and at the same time so pure and untouched.

He could see very clearly the outline of her breasts beneath the chiffon of her nightgown, but he knew that his feelings were at the moment more spiritual than physical, even though he desired her wildly as a woman.

She had aroused in him feelings of reverence and inspiration which had never happened with any woman he had known before.

It was not something that could be put into words: it was something they both knew vibrated from each to the other.

It lifted their souls towards the sky, and would, the Duke knew, make them better and finer people because they had found each other.

Zena was waiting for him to speak and after a moment he said:

"Have you any idea how beautiful you are?"

"That was what I . . . wanted you to say," she answered. "I want you to tell me how . . . glad you . . . are that I am . . . your wife."

"Let me try to put it into words, my darling," the Duke said. "I feel as if I have moved Heaven and earth to make you mine, and yet really I have done nothing. Fate did it for us."

"The fate which . . . took me to . . . Paris to find . . . you," Zena said.

She put out her hands to clasp his as she said:

"Do you realise that if we had not met in such a strange way which I know . . . shocked you . . . I would perhaps be . . . hating you at this . . . moment because you are English . . . and it might have taken me a very long time to realise that you were very . . . very different from what I . . . expected."

The Duke smiled.

"I am quite certain that the moment I saw the Princess Marie-Thérèse I should have fallen in love with her," he said, "as I fell in love with a lovely red-lipped Zena Bellefleur."

"If we are honest," Zena said, "what you felt for the girl in the next box was not the . . . love we have for . . . each other now."

"Perhaps not," the Duke conceded. "At the same time the moment I looked at you and heard your voice, something very strange happened to my heart."

"Is . . . that . . . true?"

"It is the truth," he said firmly. "But you have not yet asked me why I was in Paris and not under my own name."

"I have never had the chance," Zena answered.

The Duke laughed.

"When I see how wrapped around you were at home with chaperons, ladies-in-waiting and protocol," he said, "I find it understandable that you wanted to run away."

"I never expected that an Englishman would . . . understand that," Zena teased. "But then how many Englishmen would . . . pretend to be French?"

"What I have not had time to tell you," the Duke said, "is that my father's mother — my grandmother — was French. As you can guess she was a de Graumont."

He smiled before he went on:

"Whenever I wished to leave England, I have always stayed with one of my many de Graumont relations in France, as I used to do when I was a boy, or I have called myself *'le Comte de Graumont'*."

"So you could have fun!"

Zena finished.

"It made it possible to avoid having to spend hours of boredom at the Tuilleries Palace with the Emperor and Empress. An English Duke suffers nearly as much as a Royal Princess!"

"So, like me, you were escaping when you went to the Artists' Ball."

"Exactly!" the Duke said. "And do you know from whom on that occasion I was running away?"

"Who?"

"Somebody called the Princess Marie-Thérèse

of Wiedenstein," the Duke replied.

Zena looked at him wide-eyed and he explained:

"When I was told it was the wish of the Queen that I should marry a somewhat obscure European Princess, I was horrified!"

"You had no . . . wish to . . . marry?"

"Of course not!" the Duke replied. "I was perfectly happy as a bachelor, and although I would not pretend that I have not enjoyed many love-affairs, I had never met a woman I wanted to be my wife."

"Why could you not have . . . rejected the proposal of . . . marrying me?" Zena asked.

"You will find when we reach England that it is very difficult to refuse anything the Queen desires," the Duke said with a twist of his lips. "But I was indeed longing to defy Her Majesty and in order to think out how I would do so, I escaped to Paris."

"And what did you intend to do in Paris?" Zena asked.

The Duke's eyes sparkled as he replied.

"I will confess that I was looking for amusement."

"The sort of . . . amusement you would find with . . . a *demi-mondaine?*"

"Exactly!"

Zena gave a little cry.

"Suppose I had met you too late and you had already found someone else to amuse you like the women who dined with the Prince Napoleon, then you might never have come to Wiedenstein!"

"I had decided after I had met you that one way I could avoid being forced to marry Princess Marie-Thérèse," the Duke replied, "was to accept your father's invitation but ask if I could bring my wife to watch the *Prix d'Or*."

Zena laughed and said:

"I am so . . . glad, so very . . . very . . . glad that you fell . . . in love with me!"

"How could I help it," the Duke asked, "when not only are you the loveliest person I have ever seen in my life, but there is something more than that? Perhaps it is that we have been together in other lives or quite simply that we are each the other half of the other."

His voice deepened as he said the last word and now he bent forward to put his arms around Zena to kiss her.

Her lips were waiting for his and as he felt the softness and warmth of her body beneath his hands he drew her closer and still closer.

To Zena it was as if the Gates of Heaven opened and she stepped inside.

Thrill after thrill rippled through her until they were so intense, so vivid, that they were almost in pain.

Yet it was a wonder of wonders and everything she had longed for and prayed she might find.

Then the Duke released her and as she gave a little cry at losing him she realised he had pulled off his robe and lifted the sheet and was getting into bed beside her.

The train had come to a standstill without their realising it. Everything was very quiet and as the Duke put his arms around Zena again and drew her body close against him she said breathlessly:

"I feel . . . this is like the . . . little hut where I thought we could . . . live if we . . . ran away together, and where I would . . . look after you and . . . love you."

"It does not matter where we are," the Duke answered. "I want your love, my darling, and I will look after you now and for the rest of our lives."

He pulled her closer as he added:

"Never again, my precious, beautiful little wife, will you do anything outrageous, because I shall not only be afraid of losing you, but I shall also be a very jealous husband."

"As I shall be . . . a jealous wife," Zena said. "Suppose after we have been married for a while you . . . go to Paris to find . . . one of those . . . beautiful women whom you will . . . bedeck with jewels because she . . . amuses you?"

"If I go to Paris," the Duke said, "you will come with me. Then, my darling, I shall not go through the agonies of having to leave you at the door of your apartment."

"Was it . . . agony?"

"I wanted you and you excited me," the Duke said. "But there was something very pure about you, my darling, despite your red lips, which made me feel it was like an armour protecting you."

"Oh, Jean, you say such wonderful things to me," Zena cried, "and I am glad that I made you . . . feel that way."

"You still do," the Duke said, "and so my precious, now you are my wife I will be very gentle and will try not to hurt or shock you."

"How . . . could you do . . . that when I . . . love you and I . . . belong to you," Zena asked.

She paused for a moment before she said in a whisper hiding her face against his neck:

"I know I am . . . very ignorant and you will have to . . . tell me what a . . . man and a . . . woman do when they . . . make love . . . but whatever it is . . . because it is you . . . it will be . . . glorious and . . . wonderful . . . like when you kiss me . . . and I feel as if it is . . . part of the sunshine and . . . God."

She felt the Duke draw in his breath.

Then very gently he kissed her eyes, her straight little nose and the softness of her cheeks.

Her lips were ready for his, but instead the Duke kissed her neck and when he felt Zena quiver with the sensations he aroused in her he pulled her nightgown off her shoulder and kissed it.

His lips moved over her skin lower and lower until he found her breast.

His mouth made Zena feel so wildly excited that her whole body moved against his as if to music.

He raised his head to look down at her.

"Am I arrogant or insensitive?" he asked and

his voice was very deep and passionate.

"N . . . no . . . no," Zena answered.

"Am I cold?"

She gave a cry that was half a laugh and put her arms round his neck.

"You are . . . warm . . . marvellous . . . wonderful . . . and very . . . very . . . loving."

Then the Duke took her lips captive, kissed her possessively, demandingly and passionately. Yet at the same time there was an underlying tenderness she could not explain, but knew was even more wonderful than his kisses had been before.

She could feel his hands touching her body arousing in her unknown thrills which swept through her like shafts of sunlight, growing more and more intense until they turned from the gold of the sun to the crimson of fire.

Then as she felt the fire on the Duke's lips a flame rose within her and she wanted him to hold her closer and still closer.

She did not understand what she wanted but she knew that without it she would feel incomplete and not entirely his.

"Love me . . . I . . . want you to . . . love me," she cried. "Please . . . please . . . teach me about . . . love."

Her words made the fire in the Duke and within herself burn more fiercely and its flames leapt higher and higher.

It carried them both on the wings of ecstasy towards the heart of the sun and they were one.

We hope you have enjoyed this Large Print book. Other G.K. Hall & Co. or Chivers Press Large Print books are available at your library or directly from the publishers.

For more information about current and upcoming titles, please call or write, without obligation, to:

G.K. Hall & Co.
P.O. Box 159
Thorndike, Maine 04986 USA
Tel. (800) 257-5157

OR

Chivers Press Limited
Windsor Bridge Road
Bath BA2 3AX
England
Tel. (0225) 335336

All our Large Print titles are designed for easy reading, and all our books are made to last.